# A BIRMINGHAM THUG CAPTURED MY HEART

## SHONTAIYE MOORE

Cole Hart
SIGNATURE NOVELS

**A Birmingham Thug Captured My Heart**

Copyright © 2020 by Shontaiye Moore

All rights reserved.

Published in the United States of America.

Published by Cole Hart Signature, LLC.

**Mailing List**

**To stay up to date on new releases, plus get information on contests, sneak peeks, and more,**

*Go To The Website Below...*

**www.colehartsignature.com**

W arm, bright-red blood trickled from the cut above Zoe's eye. It was sure to leave a scar—a "beauty mark" as her mother liked to call them. "Beauty marks" were plentiful on her body. It was nothing new to Zoe, since getting kicked, punched, and slapped was the norm for her.

"Mommy please!" Zoe screamed and begged, as her mother dragged her through the carpeted hallway by a fistful of her hair.

Kicking and flailing in desperation, Zoe could feel the rug burns form on her body, while the braids that held down her once smooth, flawless weave, felt like they were being ripped from her scalp.

"Bitch, I will kill yo' little ass in here!" Nora yelled to her daughter before finally releasing her hair with an angry thrust.

She hunched over Zoe's petite, frightened body, and huffed heavily from a mixture of anger and exhaustion. Zoe glanced up at her mother. Her hair flowed silkily down the sides of her face, and although she was beautiful, her face was contorted into a grimace.

Seeing her only child terrified and balled up in the fetal position meant absolutely nothing to Nora, who was as selfish as they came. Snot and bubbles trickled from Zoe's nose, while big salty tears poured from her eyes. Despite her battered state, she stayed still on the hardwood floor, praying her mother wouldn't deliver another painful, brutal blow to her body.

Zoe squeezed her eyes shut. Hoping and praying that the darkness alone would help her escape her beating --- her reality. Every day, she secretly wished that God would take her out of her hellish world and end her life.

Before she passed, her grandmother always told her, "*God never made mistakes.*"

Zoe figured she was going through what *He* needed her to see, so she could be what *He* needed her to be.

A part of Zoe felt like she was being prepped for her calling. She was in her second year of college, majoring in Social Work. She hoped to eventually become a Child Advocate and take abused children out of the same Hell she had grown up in. It was a cold world that she hoped to someday make a little warmer for others. Fortunately, Zoe herself knew what love felt like; her grandmother had shown her each day she graced the Earth with her presence. Once she passed, the only love that Zoe had, was buried right in the dirt with her.

Memories of her grandmother were the only things that kept Zoe going. Their simple life in the country were the best years of life. Zoe considered herself lucky; some children never even got to know the feeling of love at all. Like a lot of black babies in Birmingham; she was born to a young, uneducated mother out of wedlock. A selfish young mother, with blatant feelings of resentment to her offspring and child's father.

Zoe never understood why her mother disliked her so much. It had to be because of her father. Maybe it was because she looked so much like him. Perhaps Zoe's face was a painful reminder of their failed relationship. Whatever the reason, it had to be powerful because every chance that she got, Nora treated her only child like absolute shit.

Nora looked down at her terrified and helpless daughter and felt no sympathy for her. She knew her long-time boyfriend

Bernard, known in the streets as Redz, was sleeping around with a bunch of hoes; however, she had no idea that one of them would turn out to be her own daughter.

After coming home abruptly from a trip to the hair-salon, Nora was shocked to see her twenty-year-old daughter knelt in front of her man, with his wood lodged deep in her mouth. The sight was more than enough to send her into a jealous rage. Nora didn't ask any questions. For her, there were none to ask. She automatically assumed the act she'd just witnessed was consensual — That she had been betrayed by her own daughter.

Shocked to see her home early, Zoe nor Redz could react, respond, *or* run fast enough to escape Nora's rage. The glass vase she had grabbed and hurled at Redz, slammed forcefully into the back of his head, shattering on impact. Luckily for him, the knot and cut the vase left on his head was minimal, since he had a thick patch of fat, matted dreadlocks to serve as protection.

Redz was a fat, disgusting excuse for a man; however, Nora adored every bit of him. Twelve years her senior, he took her and Zoe in when she herself was twenty-nine, and Zoe was fifteen. Beginning to experience feelings of self-consciousness due to aging, Nora felt like she had hit the jackpot when he came into their lives.

Redz owned a strip-club several towns over, and had "money longer than train smoke," as rapper Pusha T liked to say. With Redz by her side, Nora went back to being one of the baddest broads in the small city. Seemingly overnight, her lifestyle went from basic and boring, to luxurious and carefree. Gone was the tiny, two-bedroom apartment in the hood; she now got to rest her head in a luxury townhouse downtown that overlooked the river.

From simple to extravagant — everything in her life had been upgraded. Even her ten-year-old Honda Accord had been replaced with a brand-new, jet-black Mercedes Benz that had only fifty miles on it when Nora drove it off the lot. Weekly manicures, pedicures, and facials soon became her norm. As long as Nora kept Redz satisfied, there was nothing that she couldn't have.

Nora's high maintenance routines and expensive cosmetic procedures, however, weren't enough to keep Redz eyes from regularly wandering. It hurt her even more that it was someone twenty-years her junior: her own daughter. Although still undeniably beautiful, the age difference was a major blow to Nora's self-esteem. Creamy, milk-chocolate skin, eyes like nightfall, and unusually curly hair; Nora's beauty was her superpower. It was all she brought to the table, and unfortunately, she knew it. For that reason, Nora dreaded aging, and every year was a painful reminder that she wasn't getting any younger.

With her foolish and immature thought pattern, she prided herself on being able to compete amongst the baddest chick's in town --- young or old. The treacherous act she'd just witnessed a moment ago was the ultimate blow for her. Her superpower had been taken away, and the devastating jolt she felt to her already delicate self-image was immediate. Nora looked down at Zoe, pursed her lips together, and spit on her.

"I want you out my house today," she said with finality before walking away.

Although the rush of adrenaline she'd gotten was just beginning to subside, her chest still heaved up and down as she grabbed her purse off the couch and walked out the door. Nora had no clue where she was going, but she had to get out of that house. If she didn't, she was going to hurt someone.

Terrified, Zoe remained still until she heard the door slam. Struggling painfully to get up from off the floor, she shamefully and silently wiped away the thick wad of spit off the side of her face. She not only felt humiliated; she felt violated. While visible tears smeared her face, she also cried silent ones inside. Her heart was shattered. She couldn't believe her own mother would treat her in such a way. She didn't know what she had done to deserve a mother like the one she had. Even though Nora had birthed her, she seemed to despise her. Not only was she cold and unloving, she made Zoe dread her own existence.

Zoe's entire body throbbed in pain as she limped painfully slow into her room to pack her belongings. Nora had told her to leave numerous times; however, this time, she knew she meant it. She knew this day was coming. She'd known that it would only be a matter of time before her mother found out that she had been sleeping with Redz. While her mother saw her as a back-stabbing whore, it was *she* that was truly the victim. However, there was no need to even try to explain what was really going on to her mother; she knew it would do no good.

Nora had no job and depended on Redz to take care of all the bills in the house, including Zoe's tuition at Samford University. As soon as Zoe signed her acceptance letter and became legal, Redz wasted no time holding her pricey tuition over her head as leverage to get into her young panties. He knew that without his assistance, she would never be able to afford the school, and that was the exact reason he had advocated for her to attend such a pricey university, to begin with. Lost in a world of materialism, Nora had no idea Redz had been plotting on her only child since she was a mere sixteen-years-old.

Zoe had always been stick-figure skinny; however, as soon as she turned sixteen, she had basically transformed from a caterpillar to a butterfly. Out nowhere, she suddenly had round breasts poking through the baby-doll t-shirts she liked to wear, as well as a firm round ass protruding from her Forever 21 jeans.

As soon as her eighteenth birthday came, Redz wasted no time pouncing on the vulnerable and mentally abused teen. As much as Zoe wanted to tell someone and confide in her mother, she knew it was no point. Nora wasn't going to throw away her meal ticket, especially not for Zoe. In desperation and with little choice, she complied.

Whatever, whenever, and wherever Redz wanted it, he got it. At first it was multiple times a day, but it soon scaled down to once a week as he broke her young body in. As time went on, he became more and more lax about where they would meet, eventually regularly forcing her to have sex in the home the three of them shared. When Zoe protested, Redz would purposely withhold or be late with her tuition. Desperate to finish school, Zoe reluctantly allowed Redz to call the shots.

Zoe knew it was the beginning of a bigger nightmare to come. She had no place to go, and no one to turn to. Luckily for her — after playing the quiet, compliant slut for months, she would eventually persuade Redz to pay her tuition up for the year. Luckily, she had; it would now buy her some time to get on her feet. She knew that he would no longer pay for anything she needed since her mother had found out. He had already gotten what he wanted so there was no need to. The reality was, he didn't give a fuck about Zoe *or* Nora.

Zoe had never been on her own before, but she knew that today would mark the beginning of her new life. She planned to accomplish her goals by any means necessary.

## ONE YEAR LATER

Zoe sat hunched over in her living room recliner and pulled the separators from between her toes. She smiled while admiring her impressive work. She had perfectly painted her toes snowflake white and it looked almost as good as when the Asian's did it.

"Yo, how much money you make last night Candydrop?" Zoe's roommate Luscious asked her, addressing her by her stage-name. She liked to do that from time to time. Zoe would have done the same, except Luscious was the actual name that she went by all the time.

The two had met a year back during auditions at The Sugar House Strip Club: the place where all the ballers went to satisfy their sweet tooth.

"I made out okay. About a stack since the basketball game was last night. When it was over, some of the players came through and was tossing that shit left and right," she said, refer-ring to the cash the ballers liked to throw into the air to ensure a top-notch performance.

"Damn ... I knew I should've carried my ass; sick or not," she said with a dry cough she muffled with her hand.

Stretched out on the sofa, she reached down onto the floor

and grabbed a tissue out of a box she had nearby. She brought a few to her nose and blew into it, following up with a few dabs to make sure no residue was left behind. She had been coming down with a cold and it seemed to be getting worse. The cough was now accompanied with a stomachache. She hoped she wasn't coming down with the flu. It *was* that season. She wasn't about to keep letting it fuck up her money though.

"If you made a stack, I know I could have left out of there easily with three," Luscious bragged in reference to the money she could have made.

Zoe rolled her eyes in annoyance, even though she knew her friend was right. Many of the ballers that frequented the strip clubs, including the one they worked at, preferred big-booty, voluptuous women like Luscious. They were the ones that all the guys were after. It wasn't unusual for many of the girls to go on to have relations with them. That was the norm in the life of a stripper.

Those that were lucky, were pulled out of the clubs and made side-chicks to those that may have just so happened to be already boo'd up. Others who *really* hit the jackpot, were wifed up by some love-struck athlete or drug-dealer, although that was a rare occurrence.

Although surgery-produced curves, and extra-large asses were popular and attractive to most of the men that visited the club, Zoe had no desire to permanently alter her physical appearance to make more money in a profession that she was planning to soon depart from

At 5'5, 125 pounds, Zoe was considered petite. However, her small frame, caramel-colored skin, wavy hair, and honey-brown irises speckled with gold, did help her turn heads in the club, as well as appeal to those that desired a deviation from the norm. She was what some considered, exotic. She didn't make as much money as some of the donkey-booty girls like Luscious, but she was still doing well enough to take care of what she needed to take care of.

"I definitely don't doubt that," Zoe responded in agreement. "Cola's funky, ugly ass surely was killing it. The way she was acting all thirsty, popping extra hard, dem niggas had crowded around her and was flicking paper at her like it was nothing," she added, remembering the scene and how they had made it rain currency all over the bitch she despised.

Luscious rolled her eyes. Neither of the two women could stand Cola. She was their nemesis and it was always some drama going on between them. From the very first day the girls started, Cola made it clear they were not welcome, nor wanted there. Cola and Luscious especially hated each other. They had nearly come to blows on multiple occasions.

Zoe did her best to stay out of whatever beef her and Luscious had going on and did her best to stay out of Cola's way. At damn near thirty, Cola seemed as if she was making a career out of stripping and the drama associated with it. Rumor was she'd been there eight years. Zoe had one year of school left, and once that was complete, she hoped to put the life she was forced into, completely behind her.

The day her mother put her out of the house for sleeping with her boyfriend, Zoe began her hustle immediately. After searching for a job in the small city, she knew she was going to have to find a non-traditional method to get paper. The jobs that were hiring weren't enough to pay her tuition and keep a roof over her head, so she started looking in the surrounding towns.

With no luck in her job search, Zoe decided to step outside of her comfort zone and attend an audition as a dancer at The Sugar House Strip Club. She had stumbled upon it one day while searching for jobs on Craigslist. The spot was in a town right outside of Birmingham. It also wasn't too far from the club of her mother's now, *ex-boyfriend*, Redz. The Sugar House was his biggest competitor.

Although she didn't have a car and had to initially take the bus outside of the city to get to the club, that didn't deter Zoe. She figured she would give it a try since it was her last hope and shot at making some real money. Luckily for her, she did well at the audition and was given the opportunity to dance and earn hundreds of dollars a night; and that she did. And had been continuing to do so for the last year.

Although she wasn't proud of the job, it alleviated a ton of bill-related stress, as well as eased her financial load from school. Since the day her mother beat her down in their home, she hadn't spoken to her since. Zoe had, unfortunately, run into Redz after that fateful day her mother had tossed her out on the streets. She wasted no time making it clear that she wanted to put the past behind her. She acted like she didn't even know him when he came up to her smiling and trying to hold a conversation with her like she was his long-lost friend.

After telling him to kick rocks, Zoe walked away and never looked back. She had done the same with her mother. It wasn't even six months after she had put Zoe out, that Redz had in turn, rolled out on her. The last she heard, Nora was still trying to find the next man to take care of her. Zoe was glad that karma had come back and bit her in her miserable ass.

These days, she kept thoughts of her mother suppressed and pushed back to the furthest part of her mind. Considering what she'd come from, things were going well for Zoe. She had some money saved up, was scheduled to graduate in a year with honors, and shared a small, but luxury-apartment with her best-friend, *(and only)* friend, Luscious.

Luscious was ghetto-fabulous at its best. A corn-fed redbone, with a thirty-inch weave, Luscious was the epitome of thickness, Southern women were known for. Although only average looking, Luscious had a stable of men vying for her attention and she loved every minute of it.

"Well, tonight I'm gon' make sure that hoe don't make *any* money," Luscious continued, forcing Zoe's attention back to her.

"I'm about to get myself together so I can go in there and show her how a real bitch do it," she said before getting up off the couch.

"She already knows how I gets down," she said.

She playfully arched her back and made her round butt jiggle and pop up and down. Her bright red, waist-length weave shaking with it. Zoe laughed in response. Luscious was always trying to compete against someone.

"Girl sit down somewhere ... You need to be laying down and getting rid of that cold or whatever it is that got you over there looking sick," Zoe said seriously.

She didn't know if Luscious could see it or not, but she didn't look too good. Her usually vibrant skin was pale, and the lack of sleep she was getting had bags making themselves at home underneath her eyes. Zoe understood though. The hustle never stopped. They often focused more on the dollar than on self-care.

"Girl, I'm good. I'll rest tomorrow. Besides, Niko is going to be in the building tonight," she said happily, referring to one of her current love interests.

Niko was a fat, unattractive drug dealer, who happened to also be dating Cola. Of course, Cola had him first, but Luscious --- always ready to compete, had no problems stepping on her toes. The fact that it was Cola, made it all the sweeter. From the looks of things, Cola would soon be a non-factor. Niko was on Luscious' top heavy, hitting her off with money constantly, and calling her every hour.

Cola wasn't yet aware that Luscious had been seeing her man behind her back. Something told Zoe, that she would be finding out later that night.

❁❁❁

FRIDAY NIGHTS ALWAYS JUMPED AT THE SUGAR HOUSE. Tonight, they were having a live performance by a local rapper named Twists. He had just dropped a hit single that was getting major airplay. Knowing that he would draw a large crowd, the club wasted no time booking him. The girls knew that it was going to be a big money-making night. The place was jam-packed with men and women alike.

Strobe lights lit up the club's interior, while strippers gyrated and shook their ass all throughout. While they competed for the attention of the patron with the biggest bank, customers laughed, partied, and got their eat and drink on. The Sugar House was truly the place to be.

"Bitch you see all them nigga's out there. You ready?" Luscious asked, walking back into the crowded dressing room.

After doing her makeup and getting dressed, she had peeked out onto the floor to check out the scene.

"Hell yeah! Ready like Freddy," Zoe replied, as she stood at her locker and slathered a shimmery lotion all over her body.

She looked in the mirror attached to her locker and confirmed that her makeup was flawless like she'd projected. Both the girls looked like modern-day video vixens.

It was only a little after nine and all the girls were anxious to rush out and get some of that money that was circulating abundantly through the club. Twists himself, had brought a large team of thirsty niggas with him. In addition, the place was packed with locals, as well as a bunch of city-folk from the nearby city of Birmingham. Everyone had come out to show support for the budding artist that was shining light and giving their area a new sense of recognition in the hip-hop music industry.

"It's definitely some money up in here tonight. The floor gotta be at capacity ... But shit ... knowing Chris crooked ass, it's probably *over-capacity*," Luscious joked referring to the money-hungry owner of the club.

He was known for taking in more patrons than legally allowed by the local fire marshal.

"You ain't never lie," Zoe went to reply, but stopped when she was unexpectedly bumped, and damn near knocked over into a row of benches by an unknown person.

"Yo! Watch where the fuck you going!" Zoe demanded when

she spun around to see who the rude bitch was that had bumped her.

She frowned when she saw that it was Cola and her two side-kicks: Smoke and Toots. Without a doubt, Zoe knew Cola had bumped her on purpose. But for the sake of her job, she chose to let it ride. Cola ignored Zoe's remark, stopped right beside her, and instead, turned her attention to Luscious. She got within inches of Luscious' face and then proceeded to address her disrespectfully.

"Bitch, what's this I hear about you fuckin' with Niko?" Cola asked, getting straight to the point.

"Excuse me?" Luscious responded with a confused frown.

She tilted her head slightly to the side as if she hadn't heard the question. The look on Luscious' face caused Cola's blood to immediately boil. The fake-ass confused expression on her face looked more like a grin to her.

"You heard what the fuck I said. Word in Sugar House is you and Niko got something going on. If that *is* the case, then you are being really disrespectful."

This time, Luscious *did* smirk before pursing together her heavily glossed lips.

"First thing Cola ... believe none of what you hear and only half of what you see ... Trust me, sweetie, when I'm ready to show you that other half ... *I will.*"

"Bitch, I'll beat yo' ass," replied, quickly losing her patience.

"Keep playing with me. My source is very fuckin' reliable, and I saw ya number pop up in his phone the other day. You barkin' up the wrong tree hoe."

Instead of responding, an arrogant smirk crawled across Luscious' face. Cola didn't bother to say anything else since she knew Luscious would never admit to anything until she was good and ready to. It had been pointless to even approach her. All Luscious had managed to do was further antagonize her.

"Come on y'all," she said to Smoke and Toots, before walking off.

"I'm so sick of her ass," Zoe finally said after Cola and her crew walked off.

"The only reason she walks around like she Tough Tony is because her brother Ron is head of security. I swear I be ready to fuck her ass up. It's gon' be one of these days I'm going through something, and I'm gonna lose my job over that ugly, camel-looking bitch."

Zoe was heated, but Luscious was more amused than anything. Cola's brother Ron was head of security. He also happened to keep a lot of overdue and well-deserved, beat-downs from occurring. The few that had popped off on his sister, ended up terminated. There was too much money to be made to fight with Cola, so the girls ignored her and let Cola walk around thinking she was tough.

"Girl, don't even get yaself worked up over hoes like Cola," Luscious stated. "She just mad ... Mad `cuz I played her wack ass brother. Let him eat this ass and didn't fuck him. Both them been hating ever since."

Luscious stared at her reflection in the bulbed-lined mirror and adjusted her hair before continuing.

"And her ass is even more mad now `cuz she knows that I'm about to take her so-called man. That bitch acting like a real-live, dick-strung schoolgirl. That nigga's a hustler and we shake our ass for a dollar. He ain't nobodies' man," Luscious stated honestly. "That hoe know it ain't no rules in this game. Hell, she ain't my friend, and that makes him, his dick, *and* his money fair game," she smiled. "Hoe been mad ... and she gon' stay mad," she said in satisfaction.

She smoothed on another thick coat of MAC Lip Glass, before grabbing her Victoria's Secret spray off the counter and misting herself generously with it.

"She just mad `cuz she ain't me," she continued arrogantly.

"Well, I wish you would settle whatever score you have with her, `cuz she's a dumb bitch and I'm tired of it. If you don't get that shit in order soon, it's going to start fucking with our money."

Just as Luscious went to speak, the DJ announced a change of rotation. It was Luscious' turn to go up on stage.

"That's my cue," she winked, before walking off.

Before she got completely out of the dressing room she turned around to Zoe.

"And don't worry Zoe, I plan to settle the score soon. Believe me when I say, she won't be a problem much longer. Come out and watch me work bitch," she laughed, before walking off.

## 3

Like any typical night Luscious' stallion-like physique graced the stage, she commanded attention. The song by French Montana and the City Girls was especially fitting since they were in a strip club, where anyone could get lucky if they brandished the right amount of dollars.

*"I'ma bounce this ass for a rich ass nigga. I'ma get a bag, ol' gold ass digger. You can't fuck with me if you ain't got that cash. You wanna see some ass. I'll wiggle it. Wiggle it. Wiggle it. You gotta spend that shit. Spend that shit. Spend that shit."*

Luscious swayed her thick hips from side-to-side and skillfully shook her ass to the beat of the hip-hop music playing. Her now blonde weave swinging by her hips with it... She wanted her performance to be extra special; she had a visitor. Although Luscious had met her newest sponsor Niko in that very strip club, he'd never seen her perform. He'd stumbled upon her a few times; however, each time she was on the floor giving private dances or mingling amongst the others. Niko had a thing for big, thick women. With Luscious' tall, curvy body and charming personality, it wasn't long before Niko was relentlessly pursuing her. Within thirty-days, Cola was nothing more than another body to Niko — awfully close to becoming an irrelevant fling from the past.

Even though Luscious knew that dating Niko was going to cause problems between her and Cola, she still decided to rub it in her face that she'd practically stolen her man. Besides, Luscious was in her final days at the club. No one close to her knew it yet, but Niko had already told her that he would get her out of the club and take care of her. That he had other ways for her to make money. More money than she could imagine. She just hoped that Zoe was on board.

Luscious continued to sway seductively across the stage, her performance capturing the attention of nearly every baller in the building. Luscious had a way of owning the songs she danced to. She could shake her ass to the most ratchet and ghetto lyrics, yet still find a way to keep her audience mesmerized.

She glanced around the dark crowd for several minutes until she found who she was looking for: her visitor ... Niko. Biting her lip sexually, she winked at him and motioned with her finger for him to come up on stage. Lit and in a festive mood, he didn't hesitate to accept his "man-of-the-hour" invitation. Without saying a word, he waltzed right up to the stage, carrying that boss-like swag and confidence right up with him.

☙❧

AS SHE WATCHED FROM THE FLOOR, COLA COULDN'T BELIEVE the blatant act of disrespect Luscious displayed. When Luscious had motioned for Niko to join her on stage, she didn't actually think he was going to carry his fat, dumb ass up there. She'd been watching the two of them all night. She hadn't seen them together even once. She was hoping the rumors she'd been hearing were false; however, she'd seen the text-messages between the two, heard a few whispers around the club, and even saw them lingering around each other for one too many times. She had to see it for herself.

Technically, Niko wasn't her man, but she didn't care. If she was fucking him, that made him off-limits to any bitch that worked there. She had warned all the girls to stay away. She had also warned Niko that he'd better show her some respect when he visited the club. Although they hadn't been fucking around long, he knew how she felt about him. Niko had agreed that he would never disrespect her but apparently the vow meant nothing to him. He didn't care about Cola or her feelings. A man of his status was used to doing and getting what he wanted.

With anger, Cola watched as Luscious bounced her ass with extra ferocity. She had stepped her performance up big time as soon as Niko joined her on the stage. Cola understood Luscious' thirst. If she was going to bounce her ass for a rich ass nigga, then he was definitely the one to do it for. Because Niko was that: a rich ass nigga. A fat, rich ass nigga, but still a rich ass nigga, nonetheless.

With every second that passed, Cola felt her anger grow. She couldn't get over the fact of how disrespectful the two of them were. Luscious continued to grind her ass hard into Niko, while he leaned back and gripped her hips, seemingly enjoying every moment of it. In Cola's eyes, they were practically fucking on-stage.

Just when she thought Luscious couldn't get any more disrespectful, she realized she had thought wrong. Luscious dipped low in front of Niko and brought her ass back up against his pelvis. She spun around, brought her leg around his back, and wrapped her arms around his neck. To seal her performance, she brought her lips to his and they kissed passionately on the stage. While they kissed, Niko gripped her ass tightly for everyone to see and picked her up off the ground. Then ... Luscious did the unthinkable. While she tongued Niko down, she scanned the club looking for one specific face. In that crowded club, Luscious' gaze fell on Cola. When their eyes met, she stared her dead in her face and winked.

Cola was now left with zero doubt that the whole show she'd

just put on, had been done with malicious and petty intent. It was like Luscious took pride in embarrassing her. The move caused Cola's blood to boil and sent her into a frenzy.

Cola didn't remember running from the floor and up onto the stage. One minute she was watching Niko and Cola disrespect her; the next minute she had a glass beer bottle in her hand and had furiously smashed it against Niko's head.

Without bothering to see who had attacked him, Niko's animal-like instincts kicked in. He spun around, meaty hands flying, and delivered a right-left combo into Cola's face. She flew back violently off the stage, landing limply into the crowd. Seeing their girl involved in a commotion, Smoke and Toots ran to her aid. From there, things would immediately take a drastic turn.

༄

BEING HEAD OF SECURITY MADE RON THE EYES OF THE SUGAR House. Although he usually didn't patrol the floors, he still knew what was happening as soon as it happened. And something always happened at The Sugar House. Someone was always out of line. From drunk and unruly guests, to argumentative customers, to sexually aggressive customers — Ron and his team were always forced to maintain and restore order. Tonight, was a little different, however. Instead of being informed of an altercation over his walkie-talkie, he'd just so happened to be looking at the cameras, to catch the one transpiring tonight.

Ron was furious after witnessing his sister punched and manhandled. Snatching his legally permitted gun off his hip, he fled directly to the center of the chaos and to Cola's aid. No one was going to touch his sister without facing immediate consequences.

Storming into the crowd, he quickly located the person responsible for the violent attack against his baby-sister. Without uttering a word, he brought his arm up and viciously smacked the unknown man across the side of his face with his pistol. His team of security had already rushed onto the stage, shut down the performance and had the men surrounded, while Luscious did her best to scream what had happened. She tried to explain that Cola had attacked *him,* and without thinking, he reacted. Ron's arrival, however, would turn a bad situation into a nightmare.

⚜

ZOE WAS PERFORMING A LAP DANCE WHEN SHE HEARD THE commotion on the stage. She never saw Cola run up; she just witnessed the aftermath. When she looked up, Cola was flying off the stage and into the crowd. That's when all hell began to break loose. People started yelling and security came running. She watched as they approached Cola and Luscious' boy-toy Niko. He was irate and ready for battle. Security rushed to grab him but quickly found themselves face-to-face Niko's angry-looking team of goons. Niko pushed the guard that had reached for him. After a brief exchange of words, they all appeared as if they agreed for Niko and his crew to just leave. That's when she saw Ron push through the crowd, fly on stage and smack Niko across the face with the butt of his gun. What a mistake that was.

Before Niko could even react to being struck, his man closest to him, pulled his gun. With zero hesitation, he aimed it, squeezed the trigger, and shot Ron multiple times. Where Niko and his niggas were from, the type of disrespect Ron displayed caused for gunfire. They didn't give a fuck who it was. Chaos immediately erupted. Strippers and customers all began scrambling and ducking frantically to get to safety.

Although Ron was armed, not everyone on his security team was. Most of them worked at the club part-time and weren't licensed to carry. They were equipped to handle the occasional fist fight --- not a full-fledged shoot out. With Ron down, they were overwhelmed and immediately outgunned. The only thing they could do now, was seek cover.

"Luscious!" Zoe screamed desperately to get her friend's attention; however, her voice went unheard due to all the yelling and noise around them.

Zoe's eyes darted around frantically to find an escape out of the club. There was one main entrance and two emergency exits. All three were jammed pack with people pushing and shoving to get out. Zoe jumped in terror and kept her eyes glued to an escape path as Niko's crew continued to let off more shots.

"Get the fuck out the way!" Niko and his crew screamed to clear a path so they could get out of the club.

They knew police were coming and they didn't want to be around when they got there. They knew that people were hurt or likely dead. Frankly, they didn't care. The club's "so-called" Head of Security had put everyone in danger when he jumped out the window. In Niko's eyes, the violence and drama occur-ring were Cola and Ron's fault. Ron had used excessive force from the very beginning; so, out of instinct, they did the same.

As people moved out of the way in terror, Niko and his team waved their guns around threateningly until they were able to get out of the door. The moment they pushed through the door and inhaled their first breath of fresh fall air, they hauled ass to the big, black SUV they'd arrived in. Disobeying every traffic law imaginable, they peeled off into the night and sped their asses back into the gritty city of Birmingham.

## ❦ 4 ❦

"So, what's up?" Zoe asked. "Did you talk to Chris?"

Luscious sighed. She had just walked through the door, hadn't even taken her shoes off, and Zoe was already bombarding her with questions.

"No, he's not answering. He's M.I.A, and honestly, I'm probably the last person he wants to talk to. I *am* part of the reason his club is shut down," Luscious admitted.

"I went by there and the entire place is taped off and boarded up," she continued. "Along with that, there was a cease and desist order attached to the door."

"Fuck," Zoe muttered.

That quickly, their job was down the drain. However, it wasn't all Luscious' fault, and Zoe wasn't about to allow her friend to take full responsibility for the actions of others.

"It is what it is Luscious, but it isn't your fault. Chris' ass had so many violations it was only a matter of time before they shut that shit down. And the shit between you and Cola was bound to happen. It was either gon' be you, *or* someone else. Shit ... anyone for that matter. Nobody could stand the bitch. Can't cry over spilt milk though. How's Ron and the rest of the people they took out?" Zoe continued, inquiring about those patrons who had been injured during the hail of gunfire Niko's unknown goon unloaded into the establishment.

"Nobody died. Thank God. Ron still in the hospital fucked all up though," Luscious responded shaking her head.

"They said the nigga hit him twice. Once in the chest and once in the shoulder," she continued solemnly.

Luscious reached down and finally pulled off her heels and then proceeded to curl up on the sectional.

"So, what's the game plan?" Zoe asked.

It had been nearly a week since the club had been shut down, and not only was Zoe getting restless, she was also growing concerned about her sudden freeze in income. She had some money saved up, but she still had a semester of school to pay for on top of the payment plan she was currently on. She could technically afford to just pay it off; however, if she did that without finding a job right away after, she knew she would soon find herself homeless.

"Yeah, I wanted to holla at you about that," Luscious responded, unsure of how to proceed with the conversation.

"You know I'm wit going to a new club," she stated, before pausing and looking over at Zoe. "But you know that The Sugar Shack was a gem. Nowhere else around here is going to compare. Especially not those other shitholes in Birmingham. We aren't going to make the same money or receive the same treatment. That's facts. Atlanta is a two-hour drive from here, and even if we commute out there, there's hella competition."

"So, what are you suggesting Luscious?" Zoe asked, eyeballing her friend with growing curiosity.

Zoe wanted her to get to the point. She knew somewhere in her long drawn out speech, there was a point. She wanted her to hurry up and get to it.

"I say we move on to the next hustle," she replied quickly.

"And what new hustle is that?" Zoe asked.

Reality was, if there was a better way to make money, she was all for it. She wasn't dying to strip. Not only was it tiring, it was also a headache. Dealing with the men, the catty females, and pole burn was something she had no qualms about giving up. But ... the money. The money was just too good. And there weren't many options in the area that compared financially.

"Well you already know that Niko get money. He said he had a way for us to make some money ... *big money*," she emphasized.

Zoe got quiet. She wasn't expecting for Luscious to bring up a move that involved someone like Niko. She knew what type of nigga Niko was. She knew the term "*big money*," would also come with *big risks*. Nevertheless, she knew that sitting on her ass wasn't going to keep a roof over her head. She had to make moves and make them soon.

"How?" Zoe asked.

"Simple. Niko and his partner came down here to expand their operations. They need runners."

"Runners?" Zoe asked.

She wasn't sure what she meant.

"Girl don't act green. Runners ... *Drug runners*. It's easy. We would be running drugs from wherever they tell us. Probably right from Birmingham to Atlanta. A few days later, we would do it again to bring the money back. Money into Atlanta. Drugs back. All we gotta do is drive. Everything else, they'll handle. You already know I'm wit' it, but the catch for me is ... he won't let me do it unless I have a partner I can trust."

"And why is that?" Zoe asked curiously.

"Because, we would have to rotate. They don't want one person constantly on the road coming from the same city. And they want people who will eventually learn the route like the back of their hand. That way, there's less room for error. If we're a team, we could do around two round-trip runs a week. One each. But it's got to be with someone I can trust," she emphasized.

"This type of business ain't for no weak bitches Zoe," she continued. "They have to make sure they can trust the people they're working with. It's too much at stake."

"How much?" Zoe asked.

"$6k a week. $1,500 each way or $3k a trip. You get three. I get three."

Zoe sat quietly. That was a lot of money for a four-hour drive there and back, once a week. But the risk involved was significant. She already knew what came with the territory. If they got caught transporting drugs, anything in that vehicle belonged to them. Not only in the court of the law, but in the court of the streets. She knew how things worked.

"Think about it," Luscious said after noticing Zoe's hesitance. "That's a lot of money per week. For basically nothing. However, it is risky. Ball is in your court though. I don't trust anyone enough to do it with anyone else. If you're not with it ... then neither am I," she said.

Luscious climbed up off the couch and headed out of the living room and towards the hallway. Before she got too far, she spun around to Zoe.

"I'm going to take a shower. You think you can let me know by tomorrow? I know I'm asking a lot at such short notice, but I agreed to meet with Niko and his partner to go over the details tomorrow afternoon. If you don't want to do it, I need to let them know that we won't be there. If it's a go, then they want to meet you."

"Yeah, I'll let you know by tomorrow," Zoe agreed.

Although she wanted to sleep on her final decision, her mind was basically made up. She needed the money, and she didn't have many options. She was going.

❧❦❧

ZOE AND LUSCIOUS WALKED INTO THE ATLANTA International Airport the next day around noon. While Luscious' thick swaying hips led the way, Zoe trailed behind her. She glanced around, looking slightly confused. She was wondering why the hell they were meeting at the airport, out of all places. Despite her confusion, she stayed quiet and continued to follow behind her friend, assuming she would eventually explain.

"They're in there," Luscious said to Zoe with a light nudge.

She pointed to a large restaurant, that also served as a popular bar for travelers that had a little time to spare. From the looks of several menus displayed near the entrance, the place was grossly overpriced, yet conveniently nestled directly in the center of the large airport. They walked into the surprisingly romantic, and dimly lit restaurant. Luscious had been to the spot several times so she was familiar with the place. Zoe however, had never had the privilege. She glanced around the place as she walked, her eyes appreciating the rustic fixtures. The place was surprisingly large, easily holding the large number of guests that had chosen the spot for the night.

After a few twists and turns, they proceeded to the rear. As they descended upon the booth they were looking for, Zoe saw Niko's familiar face, as well as one she wasn't quite acquainted with. She assumed that was the partner Luscious had mentioned. Her eyes canvassed the top half of his body as they walked up. The man was clean-cut and *fine*. Odell Beckham with a low fade, fine. He had soft-looking wavy hair, thick bushy brows, and a full beard that was tapered neatly against his face.

*God is good*, she thought to herself, before pulling her gaze away from him. Despite his stunning good looks, the somber look on his handsome face made him appear very unfriendly She hoped he hadn't caught her staring.

"Ladies," Niko said, greeting them. He motioned for them to sit.

Luscious leaned in and gave Niko a kiss on the lips while Zoe murmured a soft hello to both men. The ladies slid into the opposite booth, and then out of habit, reached for the menu on the table.

"How you doin' Zoe?" Niko asked.

Zoe smiled in response.

"This is my cousin and partna Rocko," he continued.

*Cousin*, she thought. That was a surprise for Zoe. The two shared zero resemblance. Niko was shorter and had a burlier build, and although he ranked fair in appearance, he wouldn't necessarily turn heads. They did share the same jet-black hair and fair skin color. Rocko however, was taller, leaner, and had a more athletic build.

"Wassup?" Rocko said after his cousin's introduction.

As he spoke, he revealed a pleasant smile that Zoe wasn't expecting. As he grinned, she admired the bright, sparkly rows of teeth he displayed.

"And you've already met Luscious," Niko continued.

Luscious responded with a friendly grin.

"You can go ahead and put the menus to the side. I ordered appetizers for everyone already. I got a few of the house samplers to get started. That way, there's a variety. Rocko and I have a flight to catch in a few hours, so it'll be better if we get down to business."

"So, Luscious tells me that you're the closest thing to family she's got," he started.

Zoe glanced to her side at Luscious and gave a warm smile.

"Yeah. We're close. We met each other when we were both going through some rough points. I had hit rock bottom and was going through some personal problems, while Luscious was estranged from her family. We met at The Sugar House, became fast friends, and the rest is history."

"Oh, you work at the club too?" Rocko asked.

He was surprised. The beautiful woman in front of him didn't seem like the type to shake her ass for a dollar in a strip club.

"Zoe's in her last year of college. She danced to pay her tuition," Luscious cut in, answering for her.

She didn't want Rocko trying to put any hoe-ass labels on her friend. Zoe was a good girl. When all else let her down, she gave Luscious hope. Hope that she too would one day again, be a good woman. While struggle and hardship made most bitter, it made Zoe resilient and determined. She refused to let struggle affect anyone's perception of her character. She honestly believed that every blessing and or hardship served a purpose. Zoe was different from the average gold-digging dancer. Zoe wanted to make something of herself. She was just playing the cards she was dealt.

"Oh okay. *College girl*," Rocko responded.

"Main thing Zoe," Niko continued.

He didn't want to get too far off-topic. Every question he asked, served a purpose. "I need to know that we too, can trust you. The business that we deal in, comes with risk."

Zoe listened intently while Niko spoke. Even though she was a bit scared, she maintained a brave face. She understood the risks involved and she was glad that he wasn't attempting to sugarcoat anything so she could make an informed choice.

"We pride ourselves on making sure business runs smoothly; however, there are times when shit happens, and things don't go according to plan. That rarely happens, but if it does, I must be 100% certain that you stand firm, stay solid, and don't speak on anyone *or anything.*"

"Of course. I understand, and you have my word," she agreed.

That morning when she woke up and agreed to run with her friend, Luscious wasted no time explaining to Zoe the risks that were associated with what they were planning to do. The drug game was not only risky, it was serious and could easily turn dangerous.

"Good." Niko smiled warmly. "Then I welcome you and look forward to doing business with you."

Niko looked to Rocko and nodded his head so he could proceed to run down how things truly worked. Rocko did a quick scan to make sure no one overheard what he was about to discuss. He then looked at both women to ensure he had their attention. He wanted to address them only once, as one.

"So, my cousin Niko basically runs things," Rocko started. "I'm his right hand. He has all the connects, and he deals with all the distribution. From the top of the food chain to the bottom. He considered the Plug. All the top-level dealers in our organization get their shit from him and in turn supply the city with it. Statistically, he supplies around 30% of the drugs in Birmingham; however, there are a couple other groups of niggas in the city that supply the rest. We'd love to expand, but it's too dangerous to try and expand there in Birmingham. The gangs got the rest of that shit on lock. It's not worth the risk. We would end up stepping on toes and that would cause turf war. We don't gang bang. We are businessmen and chase paper only."

"So, where do you come in?" Zoe asked curiously as soon as Rocko paused.

"I *help* him run shit. I'm the second in command. I handle all things logistics. I'm the Regional Manager of Enterprise and I have a bachelor's degree in Business from Georgia State."

"He's basically the brains," Niko added in with a proud smile.

Zoe gazed at Rocko in silent awe. He was fine as hell *and* smart. She wondered why he chose to immerse himself in street life.

"Using my professional connections, all of our drugs go through a handful of select Enterprise branches through or designated fleet of vehicles. That rental car, moving truck, or pickup truck you see riding down the highway, may be one of ours. So, the point of all this, is we're highly organized. We take business seriously, and we expect you to do the same. One slip up has the potential to bring down everything. Understood?"

The ladies nodded simultaneously in agreement. Zoe couldn't help but feel like they were getting in over their head. Luscious, on the other hand, didn't seem to think twice about her decision. She instead salivated internally at the idea of making 12k a month for doing nothing but driving some drugs around.

"So, in a few days, you both will take pictures and get brand new fake ids. Twice a week --- depending on who's running, you'll set up a car reservation at a specific branch and go pick up like a normal customer securing a rental. The car will already be loaded and specifically reserved for you, by the person in the branch that works for us. You won't know who that person is. You'll just know that when you get that vehicle, it's ready to go. The only thing you'll have to do is drive it to the specified location. Even if you come to the destination and that vehicle is empty, you still get paid. It isn't your job to ensure the work or money is there. The only job you have is to deliver. Understood?" he asked to make sure they were all on the same page.

Zoe and Luscious nodded simultaneously. Soon after their discussion, the waiter showed up with their appetizers. While they chatted and ate, Rocko couldn't help but take frequent glances at Zoe. Not only was he attracted to her, he was curious about who she was and where she came from. Helping his cousin run a drug empire didn't leave a ton of room for dating, but if given the opportunity, he was going to make time to get to know who Ms. Zoe was. And if he wasn't given one ... he wasn't going to *make* one.

## 5

"Well, where the hell is you going, Ms. Thang?" Luscious asked Zoe, who had just come through the front door.

It was only 7:30 a.m. and Zoe looked like she had a hot date or was going somewhere important.

"I had a hair appointment," Zoe responded with a smile.

She tossed her head from side to side and did a fake twirl so her friend could admire her freshly pressed tresses.

"You like?" she asked.

"Yeah, girl. You know you cute. But answer this question ... How in the hell did you get ya hair done this early?" Luscious asked puzzled. "Who was open at this time of morning? Or better yet ... Who liked ya ass enough to get out of their bed at the crack of dawn to do yo' head?"

"My stylist did me a huge favor." She paused and then admitted. "I paid her extra. Damn!" she laughed.

"Mmm hhhm. Bitch you ain't fooling nobody," Luscious said, her voice conveying blatant suspicion. "This is your first run and you done got all dolled up for a four-hour drive. I know what you trying to do," she laughed.

"And what is that Ms. Cleo? Since yo' ass suddenly psychic," she countered sarcastically, in response to her nosey-ass friend.

"You trying to look good for Rocko fine ass. Up all early and shit getting that head done. You don't even know if he gon be at the drop."

"Yeah bitch, I know," Zoe huffed, before plopping down in the couch. "I hope he is though."

Luscious gazed at her friend. She could tell she liked him. She could sense the attraction the first day they met. They would make a cute little couple. Two college-educated people spending time together. Maybe it would be good for Zoe to get out and date. She hadn't known Zoe to date anyone or have a serious relationship since she knew her. When she wasn't working at the club, she was going to school, or she was cooped up in the house watching movies on the couch.

"Well, if it's worth anything, both Niko and Rocko were at the drop off when I got their last time. It's a cute little restaurant they co-own downtown. Maybe he'll be there this time. I would drop a hint at Niko to make sure he was there, but I don't want to throw you under the bus and have you looking all thirsty and shit."

"Yeah girl, don't do that. Maybe I'll see him, maybe I won't, but if I do, at least I'll look good," she laughed.

"Yeah, sis did a good job on your blow-out."

"Yeah, thanks. But listen." Zoe paused for a minute. She hated to give off the vibe that she was nervous or had cold feet; however, she had to get it off her chest.

"I'm kind of nervous about this run."

Luscious expected Zoe to get cold feet so she wasn't surprised when she revealed her hesitance, confirming her doubt.

"That's expected," Luscious admitted, doing her best to ease her friend's apprehension. "You've never done anything like this before. But on some real shit, it's easy money. All you gotta do is do the speed limit and drive. Niko has a bunch of runners working for him. None of them have ever gotten knocked. The cars are new — There's no reason for the cops to pull you over.

And if they do, all they're going to see is a bunch of restaurant boxes like you're delivering supplies."

"How you know that?" Zoe asked. "I thought they didn't want us snooping and looking at shit."

"Yeah, girl, I know, but I had to. Everything is right in the trunk. All lined up and boxed in regular, brown delivery boxes, with a fake ass restaurant supplier logo. Real shit Zoe. All you gotta do is turn on your favorite playlist or audiobook, and drive. Get that money. It's the easiest money you're ever going to get," she assured her.

Zoe let the words of her friend soak in. She was right. She had rent and tuition to pay. She had to do what she had to do.

"You got class today?" Luscious asked after Zoe sat silently for a few minutes.

"Na. Not on Tuesdays."

Zoe took all her classes on Mondays and Wednesdays so she would only run Tuesdays and Thursdays. Luscious would run Mondays and Wednesdays. The way Rocko had it set up, they never ran on weekends. In his opinion, it was too risky to be traveling with boxes of drugs on the weekend.

"Oh yeah. I forgot."

Luscious looked up at Zoe and studied her face. She was trying to look for any additional signs of hesitation or cold feet. Niko had told her to pay attention just in case she wasn't a good fit. He didn't need some young ass chick, freezing up while transporting his shit and possibly jeopardizing his entire operation. Zoe had never been involved in anything like this, and he wanted to make sure she was ready and could handle herself. He wouldn't hesitate to dismiss her if he felt like she wasn't ready. They made too much money in the drug game to let a rookie runner fuck it up. After massive reassurance by Luscious, Niko finally relaxed. She just hoped that advocating for Zoe was the right thing to do. Zoe was a woman of few words. Luscious knew that even if Zoe wasn't totally confident in the move, she wouldn't speak on it.

"You know you can call me while you're on the road if you need to. I can talk to you the whole ride there. I just want to make sure you're okay and comfortable."

"I know. That won't be necessary though. I'm gonna put my playlist on and enjoy the ride. Besides, I have to use the GPS on my phone."

"Right. Because they don't want us to use the GPS that's in the vehicles."

"I got this," Zoe laughed. Although nervous, Zoe knew what was up: Luscious was worried. "Trust me, I'm good Luscious. I know what I signed up for. I'm not scared and having second thoughts, and I know how to drive. I'll be fine." She gave her friend a reassuring smile before glancing down at her watch.

"Look I gotta roll. I go pick up the car in an hour so I'm gonna head out. Don't want to run into traffic."

"Okay boo. Hit me when you get to the A."

Luscious looked at her friend and breathed a sigh of relief. She didn't have any real friends she could trust. Zoe didn't realize just how valuable she was. If it weren't for her, then Luscious wouldn't have this hustle. Niko demanded she vouch for whoever she brought with her and there was no one else she could vouch for. She just hoped that something else would eventually fall through for her. Something told her that Zoe wouldn't be in this for long.

⚜

It was 8 a.m. when Zoe climbed into the passenger seat of the rental: a new model, silver Nissan Versa. For some reason, she was expecting something nicer. The checkout process for the car was the typical procedure for any rental car. The vehicle had already been reserved and the reservation had already been paid for. The only thing she had to do was show the fake id she'd been given and take the keys.

She wondered where they had the drugs hidden in such a

teeny car. It didn't seem like the ideal vehicle for drug and money trafficking. Zoe's thoughts quickly shifted to the task at hand. *Girl focus*, she said aloud to herself to quiet her thoughts. She didn't get paid to think; she got paid to drive. She tapped the address into her brand-new dummy iPhone she was also just recently given. Once google maps had her location mapped out, she started the Nissan up and began her journey to Atlanta.

As Zoe drove quietly through the small city streets, she did her best to conquer her nervousness. *Drive regular. Act regular.* Those were the only requirements for the job. After about ten minutes, she merged onto the expressway and began her two-hour drive --- three with heavy traffic. She prayed the latter wasn't the case; unfortunately, her prayers would fall on deaf ears. Since it was still early, that's exactly what she had encountered as soon as she slipped in with the morning crowd. Fortunately for Zoe, the abundance of vehicles on the road allowed her to blend in, which in turn, eased her nervousness.

"Hey, Siri. Play Beyoncé," she said aloud so that her phone would automatically generate some music for her to listen to. A few moments later and she was connected.

As she crooned along to Beyoncé's soulful voice and the lyrics she belted out, Zoe slipped into a peaceful calm that she wasn't expecting on her first trip. Within an hour of driving, the traffic lightened up and the entire drive was smooth sailing from there. After about two-and-a-half hours of driving on I-20, she was now in Atlanta, navigating her way through the hellish route to downtown.

When Zoe arrived, she parked her car into the lightly occupied parking lot. She quickly exited the vehicle and locked it up as instructed. She silently breathed a sigh of relief. The hard part was over; now all she had to do was drop off the keys to the person standing at the restaurant's podium. She looked at the small, but expensive-looking building. *Carmen's*. Whoever owned the place had done an excellent job decorating it. That was confirmed as soon as she opened the glass door and stepped foot inside. Immediately, she could tell that the place had cost a lot of money. The Spanish-style restaurant was white-linen table fancy. Very intimate and consisting of tables more suited for small party dining. Imported, Spanish palm trees adorned the corners of the room, while fine china lined the tables creating a relaxed and expensive ambiance reserved for the rich and famous.

The only thing separating the entrance from the dining area was a long wall of glass. Finally, taking her focus from the elaborate designs, she redirected her gaze to her destination. The podium was only a few feet in front of her. Standing behind it was none other than Rocko. Her day was going better than she thought it would.

⚜

ROCKO BROUGHT HIS WRIST UP TO HIS FACE AND LOOKED AT his Rolex. It was 11:15 in the morning. He was expecting Zoe to walk in any minute. He got up from the leather office chair and headed out of the restaurant's office. He wanted to be one of the first faces she saw.

"You can take a break," Rocko said to Sharell, the hostess, who stood rigid at the podium.

She was an attractive young girl that was about eighteen years old. Although she was a little dull and lacking personality, she was a surprisingly good employee.

"Oh, I'm good. I just came on at ten," she replied with a glossy smile to the handsome man she recognized as one of the bosses of her workplace.

"Well do me a favor then."

He dug in his left pocket and pulled out a crispy, fifty-dollar bill and handed it to Sharell.

"Take an early one."

She happily accepted the money and quickly responded.

"Thanks. I'll be back in thirty."

While she walked off, Rocko planted himself behind the

podium in her place. He looked around and found some menus he figured he could organize while he waited. He carefully went through each one and made sure they were all neatly going in the same direction. He glanced down at the Rolex on his wrist. Before he could confirm the time, Zoe was pushing through the front door.

## ❧ 6 ❧

Rocko's perfect smile was the first beautiful sight Zoe saw when she walked through the door. Although she was nervous when she first spotted him, that nervousness soon dissolved as she got closer. The look Rocko wore on his face was warm and friendly, and for some odd reason, he almost looked happy to see her. She grinned shyly, expecting him to look away; however, he didn't. Zoe's heart began to race as she approached the hosts stand in the front of the restaurant.

"How was your first trip?" Rocko asked.

Although this was the second time she'd been in his presence, Zoe was still in awe at how attractive he was. Maybe it was the stark contrast of black hair against his smooth light skin. Or, maybe it was the way he bit down lightly into his juicy lips when he stared at her. Whatever it was, seeing him just did something to her.

While Zoe struggled to find words, Rocko's eyes seemed to peer through her. It damn near felt like he could look deep into her soul and collect her most hidden thoughts and feelings. She couldn't help but blush from his gaze. She could tell he was checking her out; yet, he did it so smoothly.

"It was fine," she said quietly. "I didn't expect you to be

here," she admitted, although she was incredibly happy that he was.

She handed him the keys to the car. She tossed her head a little as she felt one of her soft tresses brush up against her cheek. She had checked her hair before she stepped out of the rental, so she knew she still looked good. Rocko didn't miss the move. It was the simplest of actions that turned him on. He tried to keep from staring.

"Yeah ... Well, I made it a priority to be, since I knew this was your first run and all. I wanted to see how it went.

"It went good. I was nervous at first, but after I got my playlist going and started driving, everything was smooth sailing," she admitted.

"Good ... Good. So that means you'll be staying with us for a while?" he asked.

"Yeah. Unfortunately," she said without thinking.

"Unfortunately?" he asked, making a fake sad face.

Zoe leaned her head down to laugh a little. She hadn't meant if offensively.

"Well, yeah. I say unfortunately because of the nature of the business. But I'm thankful for the move."

"Oh, okay ... Since you cleared it up."

His face changed from a fake sad face to smiling.

"Well, I think it's a good thing. Gives you and I both a chance to make new friends," he added flirtatiously.

Rocko didn't plan to keep up the game of cat and mouse long. He was interested in Zoe and she seemed interested in him. Every time he would gaze at her, she would blush and look away. She had a child-like innocence and that was refreshing to him. Most of the females he met were the complete opposite. They would match his gaze and aggressiveness with no problem. Zoe intrigued him. She was almost timid. It was odd that she danced at a strip club where confidence was mandatory; however, she seemed to lack it in true form.

"New friends sound cool," she finally responded.

"Bet," he replied, before quickly excusing himself to pass off the keys to one of the employees responsible for unloading the contents from the back of the cars.

They had a system and routine that kept things running smoothly. After a few minutes, Rocko returned and handed her back the keys.

"Look, I know you gotta hit the road to take the car back. You got anything planned when you get back to Birmingham?" Rocko asked.

He knew Zoe was a college girl and he didn't want to impose; however, he desperately wanted to see her again. Rocko was a very direct man who did his best to go after whatever he wanted. Besides, it had been a while since he had been in a relationship. He honestly missed it.

"Ummm, actually I don't," she said.

"Cool. You wanna go have a late lunch or something? I can meet you back at Enterprise when you drop off the car. I just gotta tie up a few loose ends and I'll be right behind you."

"Ummm, okay," Zoe said with a surprised smile.

She couldn't believe that he was going to drive all the way to Birmingham from Atlanta just to have a meal with her. For the first time in a long time, she was genuinely excited. She couldn't wait to get to know Rocko. Something told her that they were going to get along.

※

ALTHOUGH THE RIDE TO ATLANTA WAS SMOOTH, THE RIDE home was the complete opposite. There had been an accident on the expressway that had the highway backed up for miles. Needless to say, Zoe wasn't in the greatest of moods when she finally arrived at Enterprise and returned her car. She was tired, stiff, and highly annoyed. As she exited to wait in the parking lot, Zoe dug her cellphone from her bag and began a request for an Uber. Before she could hit submit, a shiny black G-Wagon pulled in front of her. The passenger window rolled down, and there was Rocko.

"Hey, cutie. You waiting on a ride?" he said.

Zoe smiled, and that quickly her irritation disappeared, and she became calm. She laughed and replied.

"I am. I see you're right on time. I was about to get an Uber," she admitted.

"Oh, wow. You were gon' stand me up?" he asked as Zoe climbed in.

"I was actually. If the Uber came first. That ride back was a nightmare. Just long for no reason," she complained.

She glanced at the clock. It was a little after four.

"Trust me, I know. I just drove through it as well ... It was bad ... but life is all about perception. How we look at things *and* how we respond to things."

Zoe glanced at him and couldn't help but smile. He was right. She decided she would stop with the complaining and be more thankful.

"So, where we headed?" she asked, looking out the window.

"Well, I don't know about you, but after *that* ride, I'm starving. Figured we would go get something to eat and go from there," he said, doing his best to keep his eyes on the road while stealing peeks at her.

"That's cool."

"Bet, I know the perfect place."

An hour later, Zoe and Rocko were relaxing and enjoying the beautiful view of Birmingham from a rooftop restaurant called The Yard. Located in The Elyton Hotel, it was known for its elegant global cuisine.

"You okay?" Rocko asked Zoe as she used her spoon to swirl around a mound of green mush on her plate.

She had ordered the NY Strip with Basil Potato Puree.

"Yeah, I'm a little scared to taste it," she admitted with a laugh while she stared down at the mashed potatoes that were a weird lime green in color.

She'd never seen any shit like it. Although it sounded fly on the menu, she didn't expect it to look like that when it got to her table.

"That's why I stick to what I know," he grinned.

He had the Chicken Velouté, which was basically baked chicken on top of vegetables in a creamy sauce.

"You can have some of mine," Rocko offered.

"Naaa. Thank you, but I'm good. Steak is good," she admitted.

Done playing with her potatoes, she had just shoved a buttery, soft piece of steak into her mouth.

"I take it, you've never been here before," he asked.

"Naaa," she laughed. "I'm a Mickey D's kind of girl. For now, anyway."

"Right. *For now*," he said with a wink.

Zoe couldn't help but blush. Rocko had that effect on her. She felt so comfortable with him. So, at ease. Like she could simply be herself. The whole time they ate, they laughed and talked about any and everything. Zoe spoke mainly about college life and how she hoped to work in social work in the future. She learned that Rocko and Niko were raised by their grandmother and grew up like brothers in Birmingham. She also learned that he'd been single for a while and that his last relationship had ended badly.

Although Zoe didn't like to pry, she couldn't help but inquire about why things ended badly.

"If you don't mind me asking ... what happened? Did you two grow apart?"

"We didn't really grow apart ... She just didn't understand the lifestyle that I'm in. She didn't see the need for it. I met her in college. She was smart and ambitious just like you. But ... she could be judgmental. She kept telling me to choose, but I couldn't at the time that she was asking me. I felt like I owed it to my cousin to help him with what he was trying to do. It was all taking place around the same time. The move was huge, and he needed me to help him put it into play. He was paying my tuition. It was hard for me to say no."

Zoe listened intently as he told his story.

"Well, one day I inadvertently put her at risk. Her freedom. She didn't ask me to decide after it happened because she chose for me. Straight left me. I promised myself that if I found another woman that I loved again, I would take extra care of her. Keep her away from the extra shit," he explained, referring to the lifestyle that he lived.

"I'm sure that's not always easy," Zoe said softly.

"Nah, especially because I'm usually so busy that it's probably the only world I'm going to meet a woman in. But ... trust me, when the time comes, I'm going to make sure that it happens."

Zoe smiled in approval and they changed the topic. Although their conversation was over, a part of her couldn't help but wonder who this woman was that had Rocko's heart. After their meal, Rocko insisted on taking her to a jazz lounge in nearby Bessemer, Alabama after learning that she had never heard of his favorite Jazz Musician, Miles Davis. Although Rocko loved hip hop, he was a huge jazz fan, having heard his grandparents play it throughout the house most of his life. Zoe had really listened to any jazz at all, let alone, live jazz.

Despite being newly introduced to the music genre, Zoe had a blast at the charming little establishment he took her to. There were a lot of white people, which shocked her. Rocko didn't look like the type that could mingle amongst a bunch of white people. However, they had a great time, had a few drinks, and Zoe even got to twirl around with the old guy that was performing that night. They stayed all the way until closing time. Even though it was late when they made their exit, Zoe couldn't help but sulk because the night was coming to an end. She was enjoying it too much. They'd been together for hours, but she wanted more.

"I had so much fun," Zoe admitted. "I wish the night didn't have to end."

"It doesn't," Rocko replied with a grin, as they were walking out the doors of Gip's Place and were headed to Rocko's truck.

Rocko couldn't even lie, he was happy that she had expressed what he felt as well. He too was enjoying her company and wasn't quite ready for the night to be over.

Zoe smiled sheepishly. She didn't expect him to reply with an alternative.

"You could stay with me," he added.

"Stay with you?" she frowned slightly.

They reached Rocko's truck and she waited for him to unlock the door so she could climb in.

"Yeah, stay with me. It doesn't have to be my crib. We can stay at your crib. Or I can get a room. I'm not asking you to do anything ... Just hang out. I enjoy your company. I honestly just don't want the night to end so soon," he admitted.

Hearing the doors of the G-Wagon unlock, Zoe grabbed the handle and climbed in.

"Okay," she said simply.

The liquor had her feeling carefree and she felt like taking a chance. Besides, she liked Rocko, and she'd never had a real relationship. A buried part of her welcomed one with the right person. She wanted to see where things would eventually lead.

❂

ROCKO AND ZOE ENDED UP BACK AT THE ELYTON WHERE THEY had dined earlier that evening. Luckily for Rocko, it was a weekday and there were still rooms available. The hotel was one of the most expensive in the city, *and* one of the most luxurious. The 1,300 square foot, presidential suite had cost Rocko over a grand for just one night. However, to him, it was worth every penny. He honestly didn't mind a bit. He wasn't necessarily trying to impress Zoe with the lavish suite; he just wanted her to be comfortable if she decided to stay her first night with him. The suite held a separate king-size bed and bathroom in a private bedroom. That way, Zoe had the option to lock the door while Rocko stayed in the living room. He didn't want her to feel like she was under any pressure at all.

Rocko had never stayed in their most expensive space, but he was impressed when they entered. It was modern, sleek, and immaculately clean. Zoe also walked around observing the massive space in awe. Big enough for four people, the bed was draped in the thickest, finest linen, while splashes of pale yellow and smoke gray drapes and accessories made the room festive and airy.

"This is really nice," Zoe gushed, her eyes darting around and soaking in the scene.

She'd never been anywhere as nice. The apartment she lived in with Luscious was the nicest place she'd ever been.

"Yeah, it is," Rocko agreed, before sitting down in a comfy recliner close to the window.

From where he was seated, he could take in the beautiful, starry scene of the city.

"Come look at this," Rocko called out to Zoe.

Now barefoot, she crept over to where he was seated and looked out the window.

"It's gorgeous. Just as beautiful as the rooftop view from earlier."

She continued gazing out the windows at the stars sprinkled throughout the sky. Rocko couldn't help but notice a longing look in her eyes. A look like she was searching for something but was unsure of what it was.

"I could get used to this," she admitted, before walking over and plopping down on the bed.

Her body sunk into the plush bedding.

"This too," she smiled staring up at the ceiling with its fancy, spherical shaped light fixtures hanging down.

"Yeah? Well, that's good. Because I want you to," Rocko said unexpectedly as he rose up from where he was seated and walked over to sit beside her on the bed.

"Want me to what?" she asked.

"Get used to it."

She gave him a half a smile in return. *It would be nice*, she thought to herself.

"I like your style, Zoe. Humble and appreciative. You remind me of ---"

"*Who*? Your ex," Zoe asked intercepting his statement while rolling her eyes.

"Nah. Not at all. Actually ... I was going to say, my grand-mother. She was always so humble. So appreciative. Wouldn't take anything from me or my cousin Niko unless she absolutely needed it ... and that was rarely. She used to always tell me: *I don't love you for what you got. I love you for who you are*," he said, doing his best impersonation of his grandmother.

"Those type of women become harder and harder to find. Nowadays all these chicks worry about is how much money you have and what you can do for them."

"Yeah, you're right about that. But there are still some good ones out there," she assured him.

"I know," he said confidently. "I think I found one."

Rocko leaned over to where Zoe was laying and boldly pressed his lips down into hers gently. Even though they'd been out all day, she still smelled clean and sweet. He took a deep breath and inhaled her scent. Feeling her soft lips up against his caused his manhood to harden. Rocko took a moment and stared at Zoe. She had no idea how rare she was. That innocence. Those sparkling brown eyes. She was completely unaware of her beauty. She had no idea the kind of power she could yield. He had to have her.

Pulling away from Rocko's kiss, Zoe licked her lips and savored the taste he left behind. She'd entertained a few thirsty niggas, but she'd never had a man of her own. She'd never truly desired one; however, since she'd met Rocko, she was viewing men more and more differently by the day.

"Umm, I'm gonna go take a shower."

She sat up and scooted out the bed. As she walked off, she did her best to get her raging hormones in check. If they kept it up, there was no telling what was going down.

⚜

Zoe had her eyes closed and was enjoying the hot, stream of water flowing down her body, when she heard a knock at the bathroom door.

"Rocko?" she called out.

"Yeah it's me," he paused, before appearing outside of the glass and marble shower area.

A part of Rocko knew he was moving a little fast, but another part of him urged himself to go for exactly what he wanted ... And he wanted Zoe. That kiss had done something to him. And the way she lit up after, told him that she wanted it more than he did.

"I wanted to see if you wanted company," he asked.

Rocko's heart hammered in his chest while he waited for a response. He didn't know why, but Zoe had him fired up, but still scared like a little ass schoolboy. Like he'd never had any pussy before. He was *too* excited. That excitement would intensify when she did the unthinkable and responded.

"Yeah. You can hop in."

Rocko wasted no time grabbing one of the washcloths from the rack and walking into the shower. He lathered his cloth up and began washing his body from head to toe, with Zoe doing her best to steal peeks when he wasn't looking.

*Bitch, you grown as fuck. Stop acting young,* she told herself. She hated that her shyness was causing her to hold back. And for some reason, she didn't want to hold back.

Zoe had only been with one man, and that was Redz. The excitement and tingling sensation raging through her body was all new to her. She'd never had those feelings when she was with

Redz. She usually felt disgusted and as time went on, she forced herself to feel nothing.

She really liked Rocko. With alcohol coursing through her system, Zoe did something totally outside of her character and decided to turn it up a notch. Rocko had the rag between his legs, washing away, when Zoe reached down and took it from him.

"Let me do it," she said, while leaning in and kissing him passionately.

Rocko knew it was the alcohol that influenced Zoe's bold behavior; however, he decided that he would savor the moment. While her lips were still pressed against his, he slipped his tongue in and out of Zoe's mouth while she moaned in satisfaction. She had dropped the rag to the floor and glanced down at Rocko's erect dick as it pressed against her stomach.

"I want you," he whispered into her ear, as he took turns kissing and sucking the side of her neck.

Zoe didn't respond, but the look in her eyes gave him all the approval that he needed. He hoisted her up by her legs and pinned her gently against the shower wall.

Zoe moaned softly as he found her entrance and then took his time easing in and out of her. When Rocko first entered her, she wasn't prepared for his length and girth. But as seconds passed, her body conformed and welcomed him. The pain soon subsided and became pleasure.

It took everything in Rocko to contain himself. She felt so good. Her slick, tight walls wrapped around his manhood like a glove. The way she whimpered and called out to him, made him feel like he was about to lose it. *Fuck*, he moaned aloud. Her pussy alone convinced him that she was a rare commodity. As tight as the fit was, he could tell that she hadn't had too many visitors. He planned to be the only visitor from this point out. She was officially his.

Rocko knew there was probably no such thing, but everything about her was as close to perfect as it could get. He continued to stroke in and out of her, leaning in occasionally to suck at her neck.

Zoe was too caught up in the moment. She'd never felt that type of pleasure before in her life. She knew it was a dangerous move, but she was instantly hooked. Sex with Redz had always been forced and done out of necessity. With Rocko ... it was different. Electrifying.

She gripped the back of Rocko's head and brought her mouth onto his. His lips melted into hers and sent ripples through her body. In turn, her body surrendered to him.

She bit down on her bottom lip and moaned in pleasure as he continued to dig his dick deep inside of her. Feeling her soft fingers rub into his strong back, caused Rocko to pick up speed. Finally, unable to hold back any longer, he released himself into her.

"Fuck," he muttered, while he shuddered in extasy, before finally pulling himself from her.

"*Shit*," she muttered, finally coming to her senses. They hadn't used protection and he had came in her.

She picked up her rag from where she had laid it down and began to wash away their mixture of fluids from her body.

"You okay?" Rocko asked before leaning down and kissing her again.

She smiled. "Yeah, I'm fine."

"Good."

Rocko got out of the shower and dried himself off. While he waited for Zoe to finish, he sat on the couch, rolled up a blunt and took it to the head. Smoking weed was a new habit he had picked up from his cousin, but he had to admit, he liked it. Despite what people said, smoking helped him think longer and harder.

When Zoe finally emerged from the bathroom a half hour later, Rocko was all smiles. He watched her as she sauntered into the living room. With her curly hair still damp from the shower, she looked bare-faced and beautiful.

"Wassup gorgeous?" he asked softly. "You okay?"

"Yeah, I'm fine. Why wouldn't I be?"

She figured he was wondering how she felt about him and what had just taken place in the shower. Especially since she had been drinking when it happened.

"Just checkin," he assured her.

As Zoe headed to the bed, she went to walk by him, but he grabbed her arm gently and pulled her into him.

"You know you mine's right," he told her with a devilish grin.

As Zoe slid into Rocko's lap, he kissed the side of her neck. She turned her head and returned the kiss to his lips. It was something about the way that he declared it.

"Is that right?" she asked, a sweet smile creeping onto her face.

"Hell yeah. I gotchu. I'm gon' look out for you."

Zoe knew he meant well, but she didn't need a nigga to look out for her. That's not what she was looking for.

"Nah, we gon' look out for each other," she declared.

A chill swept through Rocko. She was one he couldn't let get away.

## 7

The next morning Niko called Ms. Mattie's phone for what felt like the hundredth time and left what seemed like the tenth voicemail. Ms. Mattie was an older lady that worked for him, but for some reason, he hadn't been able to get ahold of her for the past few days. It wouldn't have alarmed him as much if she were ... say perhaps, his babysitter or housekeeper; however, she was one of his most loyal runners that regularly ran several dozen kilos per week. She had been with them since day one and her going missing in action made him extremely nervous.

Still getting no answer, Niko shoved his phone back in his pocket and hopped back in his truck where Rocko was sitting quietly. They never spoke on the phone inside of the vehicle. Anything pertaining to drugs, or involving drugs, *or* involving people who they did drug business with, was always outside. They never knew who was listening.

"You get through?" Rocko asked as soon as Niko planted his bottom on the seat.

"Nah."

Rocko didn't respond. He knew what the next step would be. Someone was going to have to go look for her. That someone would have to be either himself or Niko. Rocko personally didn't feel like going to do it since he had already told Niko numerous times that they should take Ms. Mattie off drug runs. She was damn near pushing seventy. *But* ... Niko was the boss, and he felt that despite her age, she was still one of the best for the job. Now, here they were. Ms. Mattie had been unreachable for nearly three days. They hadn't heard from her since she was on her way back from a run from Atlanta to Birmingham. A run where she was carrying $100k in the trunk.

"What's next?" Rocko asked.

Niko looked at him but didn't respond. He started up the Tahoe they were in and pulled out of the parking lot. After driving for a few minutes, Niko merged onto the expressway. Rocko now knew where they were headed. They were going to Ms. Mattie's house, together. He sighed silently. That was the last place he wanted to be headed to, especially because he had been told his cousin that she was going to soon become a liability rather than an asset. In his opinion, niggas with hard heads should be able to clean up their own mess. Niko was no exception. Additionally, he had made plans with Zoe. Without little movement, he glanced down at his watch. It didn't look like his day was going to happen. Since that was now canceled, he figured he might as well get comfortable and enjoy the drive as best as he could.

ZOE WALKED THROUGH THE HALL AWAY FROM HER FINAL CLASS of the day. Her instructor had closed out their day's discussion about toxic relationships with parents, and its direct correlation to expectations in adult romantic relationships. She thought about the paper she had to write about over the weekend. She expected the paper to be easy and actually interesting. Over the years at Samford University, she'd learned that most adults seek what they lacked as children in romantic relationships. She knew that to be true firsthand. Her mother didn't protect her, love her, or show her any attention, that is what she was likely to seek from her romantic counterpart.

The problem was that although that's what most sought, it wasn't what most received. The same neglected child would accept some form of abuse as an adult in order to have that neglected need met. They would accept an occasional beatdown, accept verbal and emotional abuse, all for affection if that's what they lacked. *Why* was the question. Zoe never could understand it; it never made sense, but she knew it was true. That was one thing she feared the most. Settling, accepting, and being taken advantage of because of her mental insecurities acquired as a child. She knew she wanted to be a Social Worker, but she often wondered if she should be a Child Therapist or maybe a Psychologist. It wasn't enough to pull a child out of an abusive home; they oftentimes needed help achieving mental health. Zoe knew she had a purpose and she was so excited to one day be of service to children who had upbringings like herself.

After walking the large campus for nearly ten minutes, Zoe finally reached her car. Once she got in, she checked her phone for the thousandth time. She sighed in disbelief and threw her phone back down on the seat. Nothing. She had been hoping to hear from Rocko. A call, text, or any damn thing. She knew his ass was full of shit, just like his cousin Niko. She felt like such a fool. He hadn't called her or text her back since last night. He was supposed to take her to lunch after classes and he was a no-call, no-show. She should've known that he was going to do nothing more than get what he wanted and discard her like he probably did anyone else.

Zoe sighed sadly. *Fuck it*, she thought as she headed home. There was no need crying over spilt milk. She was used to being disappointed. Besides, she had homework to do and a paper due that she could use her time preparing for. She really like Rocko, but she wasn't about to chase him. She was done begging motherfuckers for love.

## 8

"Come on bitch. Spill the beans."

The tables had turned and this time it was Luscious who wasted no time bombarding Zoe with questions as soon as she walked through the door. Zoe had stayed out all night after her run to Atlanta and now she was just waltzing her ass up in the house like she wasn't going to have some explaining to do. As nosy as she was, Luscious wanted all the details. Every juicy one of them.

"What?" Zoe let out a nervous laugh as she began unloading her belongings to get situated.

"Bitch, don't what me! Do you know how scared you had me at first? I called your phone a million times and you weren't picking up. Thinking something happened, I called Niko and asked him if you had checked in, and he said 'yeah.' He told me don't worry and you were with Rocko. Now ... spill the motha-fuckin' beans," she demanded from her seat on the living room recliner.

Zoe sighed and plopped down on the couch. The look she gave her friend was part happy, yet partly sad.

"What's the matter?"

"I'm confused as fuck."

She pushed off her shoes and brought her feet and legs up on the couch so she could cuddle against a pillow.

"The night was so fucking bomb. I felt like a princess ... and I never felt that way with any other nigga before."

She then proceeded to tell her how the night transpired.

"I did the run. We started talking and he came at me hard. Asked me out for lunch and then followed me back to Birmingham. He was on point and sweet. Took me to a beautiful rooftop restaurant ... then a jazz club. We clicked so well."

She paused briefly.

"I don't understand it ... We went back to his hotel room and the next thing you know, shit happened."

"You fucked him?" Luscious asked, the look on her face like one of shock.

As stiff as Zoe acted when it came to men, Luscious didn't expect it.

"Yeah," she admitted in a near whisper.

"Damn bitch," Luscious replied in disbelief.

"I know. I shouldn't have," she shook her head sadly. "The first date."

She swallowed the hard lump that was forming in her throat. She was so disappointed in herself that she wanted to cry.

"So, what's going on that has you confused?" Luscious asked like a concerned big sister.

She had a feeling that she already knew what her friend was going to say.

"He was supposed to meet me for lunch, but he didn't hit me up. I haven't heard shit from him since he dropped me off this morning to my car."

"Did you call him?"

"Yeah of course. I called him and I texted him, but he isn't responding at all. I have no missed calls, texts, or voicemails. I feel like a fool," she sighed sadly.

Luscious wasn't going to beat Zoe in the head with the "I told you so's." She'd fucked plenty of niggas on the first date. She just thought Zoe would know better than that and would make better choices than her. Fortunately, Luscious never had to deal with a nigga not hitting her back after sex. Even if it was on the first night. Most of the time it was the other way around. She was the one not responding, and the nigga was blowing up her phone. Her heart went out to her friend.

"Awwww, Zoe. Well, I'm sure you'll hear from him soon," she did her best to assure her.

"Yeah, maybe," she shrugged.

"Can I ask you a question? If you don't mind," Luscious asked with a serious face.

"Yeah, girl. Go ahead," Zoe replied

"How was the dick?" Luscious sat there and eyed Zoe, waiting for a response.

Zoe let out a colorful laugh. Her friend sure knew how to lighten the mood.

"Sooooo?" Luscious urged her to answer.

"It was bomb. He did his thing. That's all I'm gon' say."

"Ohhhhhhhh," Luscious squealed. "I figured that. Niko ain't no slouch either. That nigga damn sure handles his business when it comes to laying that pipe down. You know what they say, *the apple doesn't fall to far from the tree.*"

"Sure doesn't," Zoe replied solemnly.

Unfortunately, she didn't mean that in a good way.

🖎

IT WAS AFTER MIDNIGHT WHEN NIKO AND ROCKO WERE DONE taking care of business. They had traveled all the way to Homewood, Alabama to drop in on Ms. Mattie, only to discover that she had had been hospitalized from a massive stroke. It happened right behind the wheel while she was driving. One minute she was fine, and the next minute she was having a stroke. The ending result was her veering off the road and landing nose down in a ditch.

It took everything in Rocko not to say, *I told you so*; however, due to the gravity of the situation, he refrained from doing so. The rental car had been impounded after being winched out, and it took them nearly half the day to figure out where it had been towed to. Luckily for the two, there weren't many tow trucks servicing the area where she had been found. Rocko took care of all the paperwork and finally, after most of the day was gone, he had the rental being delivered back to the agency.

As Niko and Rocko headed back to Birmingham, they silently breathed a sigh of relief. As many police officers on the scene of Ms. Mattie's crash, they neglected to search the vehicle. The 100k in cash she was transporting was still all there, neatly bundled in rubber bands and wrapped in plastic. Niko contributed their good luck to her age. There wasn't anything suspicious concerning the circumstances behind the crash so the cops who arrived at the scene weren't eager to search. Rocko however, felt a different way.

To Rocko, the situation was a loud example of their poor choices. Due to her age, Ms. Mattie should have been off the road. What if the police had searched the vehicle to look for something as minor as an identification card? They could have found the cash and Ms. Mattie would have been questioned the moment she opened her eyes from her hospital bed.

Rocko had made plenty of money with his cousin. He knew that very soon; he would have no choice but to end their business relationship. Niko's calls weren't always the best ones; yet, he still called them. That was all good, except when those bad calls were made, they could potentially bring down him as well. That was a risk he couldn't take. He had too much to lose.

After driving for a while, Niko and Rocko arrived back in the city. Niko pulled up to Rocko's condo to drop him off, but Rocko decided he wasn't letting him off the hook that easy. They needed to talk.

"Hop out. I need to rap to you really quick," Rocko stated.

Niko turned off the truck and got out. "What's up?" he asked.

"So, Ms. Mattie's out?"

"Of course. She had a stroke nigga. She done," Niko said.

The question was a silly one. Rocko had a way of getting under Niko's skin. He liked to ask questions he already knew the answers to.

"Moving forward, we gotta make better choices. She should have been out. What if the cops had searched the trunk? What if the tow company had found the money?"

"Why the fuck you keep saying, *what if* nigga? They didn't."

"It doesn't matter Niko. We always gotta stay one step ahead. We always gotta be prepared for the *what if*. We need runners we can trust and runners that are also reliable."

"I know that," Niko replied in annoyance. "That's why we just got two new ones."

When Niko had left the city and began frequenting strip-clubs in small towns, he did so with intention. Intention on finding someone that wanted money and he could train to be loyal. Bitches in the strip-clubs always wanted an out. They were always looking for a nigga, hustle, or come-up to take them out of there. No one wanted to strip forever. For that reason, Niko would look for a stripper, who oftentimes had something working against them. Most of the time, that something was age. Someone who was about the dollar but was growing tired of that life.

Initially, he thought he had found that with Cola, until he learned that she was too unpredictable and would be more of a liability than an asset. Once he hooked up with Luscious, he knew she was the one. He'd go on to charm her, spoil her a little, and then present to her an idea to get her out of the club. "*Get money with ya mans,*" is how he kicked it. "*Only weak ass bitches want to sit around and let a nigga just take care of them.*" And that's how he had run game on countless females, turning them into drug-runners who foolishly believed they were his girlfriend.

Those types of females were loyal to a fault. If they got jammed up, they'd likely never tell. They'd take their charge like a big girl and go sit down in a Federal Penitentiary for a man like Niko. As soon as their sentence started, Niko would seemingly disappear off the face of the Earth.

"Doesn't matter if we got two new ones or not. We can't keep switching up runners every time you turn around. We're going to have to find a different way to transport. That way we're working with less people. Less room for slip-ups."

"Yeah, I know. You're right." Niko finally agreed with his cousin there.

They did need a different method of transporting their drugs and money. He was looking into that.

❦

Zoe tossed and turned in her bed until finally, her eyes slowly fluttered open. She peered around, slightly confused. Then she realized what had woken her out of her sleep. She looked to her side and saw her phone vibrating around on the nightstand. With the covers slipping off her arms, she reached over and grabbed it. She had twenty missed calls. She sat up straight in her bed and wiped her eyes. She unlocked her phone and slowly viewed her call log. Rocko had been calling and texting her non-stop. She scanned her messages. Most of the messages were of him apologizing and begging her to talk to him and answer the phone. She sighed, put her phone back up on the nightstand, and laid back down. It was well after 1 a.m. and she just wanted to get some sleep. She had a run to do in the morning.

Before she could make herself comfortable, her phone began vibrating again. She quickly grabbed it. It was Rocko again. She slid the answer button over and answered it.

"Hello?" she asked, doing her best to conceal her groggy state.

"Zoe!" He was happy that she had finally answered his call.

He suspected she had been ignoring him, but as soon as he heard her voice, he realized that she probably had been sleep. He didn't want to take up too much of her time. He just wanted her to hear him out.

"Yea," she replied nonchalantly.

"Look Zoe baby. I'm sorry I couldn't meet you like we had planned. I would never stand you up," he admitted desperately. She had something special. Something that he needed. He had just gotten her, and he didn't want to lose her.

"Yea. Well what happened?" she asked. She wanted to believe what he was saying, but she knew that guys like him could lie with ease. "How come you didn't call ... Or pick up the phone ... Or call me back," she demanded to know.

She sat back up, now fully awake. She wanted to hear what he had to say. His excuse.

"I wish I could tell you, but I can't. I had last minute business I had to handle. Some real important shit going on that couldn't wait. Certain things require me to turn off my phone. You understand," he asked, praying that she did. "By the time I turned it back on, it was late. I'm sorry," he said with sincerity.

Something about his voice eased her worries. Perhaps it was the panic she sensed in his voice when she answered. Or maybe his humble pleas that had a hint of desperation in them.

"I understand," she said. "Next time just shoot me a text and give me a heads up. I get that some things in your life, I can't and won't be privy to; but please don't make me feel unwanted or rejected. That's all I ask," she said softly.

"Thank you, baby," Rocko said, with relief. "I'm sorry you felt that way. I'll make it up to you okay. Now you lay down and get your rest. I can sleep now as well," he admitted.

She smiled, said goodnight, and ended the call. Rocko was so different ... She hoped.

## ❧ 9 ☙

Zoe and Rocko's relationship blossomed quickly, with the two of them becoming nearly inseparable. Rocko admired her beauty, strength, and intelligence. He also loved the fact that she was always appreciative and even though Rocko had plenty of money, Zoe still made dedicated moves to get her own. Although he admired the quality, he wasn't fond of the fact that she still wanted to work for his cousin as a runner. Undisputedly, it was a conflict of interest. After making subtle attempts at discussing the issue, Rocko decided he had no choice but to approach it directly.

"Babe, I don't want you running," he stated out of the blue to her one day while they were laid up in his king-size bed watching Martin re-runs.

"Huh?" Zoe asked, lowering her gaze from the television. "What are you talking about?"

She sat up and turned to face her man. She had heard him, but it came so random that she needed him to elaborate on it more.

"I don't want you running drugs. It's dangerous and I'm just not with it no more," he said firmly.

He had always told himself that when he found another

woman that he wanted to spend, *or could imagine spending* his life with, he would make sure that his line of work would not destroy what they had. Even though Zoe had stepped into the drug world on her own, he didn't want her to be a part of it any longer.

"Oh, but it was okay before," Zoe responded with an eye roll.

"I didn't know you then Zoe. I didn't care about you like I do now. You weren't my girl then. Should I go on?" he asked since she seemed to need validation behind his request.

"Things changed," he continued. "I love you and I don't want to see anything happen to you. Flat out, you don't need to do it. Hell, you don't even need to work. I got you. Just go to school, take care of yourself, and take care of me. Let me handle the ugly shit."

Despite how wonderful it should have sounded, Zoe wasn't feeling it.

"I don't know if I'm with that. I don't want anyone to take care of me. I prefer to take care of myself."

"I'm ya man. A man is supposed to take care of a woman."

"Yeah, but at what cost?" she asked. "I watched my mother go through a bunch of bullshit just so she could keep a nigga taking care of her ---"

"Zoe ... Please don't compare me to no other nigga," Rocko replied sharply. "This isn't about control," he started.

For some reason, Zoe continuously forgot that he too was a college graduate. Every rebuttal she had was some type of psychological assessment. Some logical stance to argue her reasoning behind certain things. She didn't want a man taking care of her because she didn't want anyone to be able to control her with financial support. She didn't want to grow dependent on it. He understood. He got it. He had no choice since she constantly drilled it in his head. He understood her position completely, but he wasn't trying to hear it at the moment. This was much bigger than control. He didn't want her running drugs. He didn't want her risking her life, freedom, and future to take care of herself. He'd rather do that. And while he did it, he intended to set her up nicely. Put her in a position where she would be cared for forever. It was for her benefit. He had her best interest. Zoe, however, couldn't completely grasp that.

"Nobody is trying to control you. Not now. Not later. I just don't want you up and down the highway with drugs or cash. If you want to work, why don't you work at your school? Volunteer or something. Be a fucking waitress, shit. Be whatever the fuck you want! But not a drug runner!" he argued, sitting up in the bed so he could face her.

Zoe pushed her body back against the bed and threw her head back in defeat. He was right. She just wasn't sure if she was ready to depend on him fully. She also couldn't help but think how this would affect Luscious. She didn't have another source of income at the moment, and Niko wasn't going to take care of Luscious like Rocko would her.

"If I back out, what is Luscious going to do?"

"You can't worry about that. She a grown ass woman. Y'all been doing this shit for months. She should have some money saved or something."

Zoe doubted that. Luscious had expensive taste, and at three grand a week, there wasn't much left to save.

"Look, babe. Stripping is one thing. That shit is legal. Running isn't. You're about to graduate college and anything can happen. If something goes wrong and shit pops off, everything you've worked for your entire adult life goes down the drain. That's not what I want for you. That's not what *you* want for you. You gotta quit it," he said with finality.

Despite her total opposition to quitting, Rocko was right. Zoe knew he was right. It was risky and she knew it when she took the job. She was desperate and she needed the cash. So far, the reward was outweighing the risk. However, just like Rocko, Zoe knew that it eventually had to come to an end. After a moment of silence, Zoe finally replied quietly.

"Okay, Rocko. You're right, and you win. But, let me do a few more runs."

Rocko went to oppose but Zoe quickly cut him off.

"Hear me out. Let me do one last run so Luscious can get paid one last time from it. Niko isn't going to let her do it without a partner right."

Rocko sighed but nodded in agreement.

"So, once I'm done, she's out to. I gotta give her a heads up. So, she can get some other type of work lined up. Okay?"

"Okay babe. Two last runs. Then you're done. I'll let my cousin know."

Zoe sighed but nodded in agreement. Now all she had to do was break the news to Luscious.

ALTHOUGH SHE WAS HAPPY FOR HER GIRL, LUSCIOUS COULDN'T help but to feel a small twinge of jealousy when Zoe came with the news that Rocko was pulling her out of the drug running business. On one hand, she was happy that Rocko was in love with her girl and wanted to take care of her. Lord knows if anybody deserved happiness, it was Zoe. However, on the other hand, she wished that Niko felt the same way about her.

After hearing the news, she smiled brightly and hugged her friend. A mixture of emotions ran through her. She wasn't sure if it was from the news or the fact that just earlier that day she'd learned she was pregnant. It was her first pregnancy, but she'd heard that it had your hormones all over the place.

"I'm happy for you, girl. You deserve it," Luscious said with genuine intent.

"Rocko's going to tell Niko so neither of us have to. See if maybe he can find someone to replace me as your partner *or* maybe just let you do it alone a few days a week."

Luscious didn't reply right away. She sighed and sat down on the closest chair.

"Yeah, I doubt it. And besides, it's time for a new move."

Zoe sat down on the sofa across from her. She looked at her friend with worry.

"You okay?" she asked.

"I'm pregnant," she said softly.

Zoe's hand flew to her mouth to suppress the gasp.

"Girl!"

Zoe couldn't contain her excitement. However, she had to, at least for the moment. She didn't really know how Luscious felt about expecting.

"How do you feel about it?" Zoe asked.

"Honestly. I'm kind of happy," Luscious beamed but then her happiness quickly dissipated. "But ... I know Niko's not going to want it. Not by me anyway," she admitted. "I stripped and he was cool with it. I run his drugs and he's still cool with it. Meanwhile, he fucks me and has no desire to put me in a better position, so I won't have to do either of those things. He shouldn't want me to do those things. Because he has no problems with me doing those things, tells me one thing: he doesn't care about me. He's definitely not going to want me to have his baby."

"So, what are you going to do?" Zoe asked.

"I'm not sure yet. I'd love to have it. But a part of me knows I'm not ready. Not financially, anyway."

"Well, you know I support you no matter what."

"I know, lovebug. And I love you for that."

"Oh!" Zoe reached in her pocket.

She almost forgot something. She was glad. The conversation was turning somber and she wanted to give something to help brighten up her friend's mood.

"I'm moving in with Rocko in a few weeks. Over winter break."

While she dug in her pocket to retrieve what she'd forgot, she noticed the look on Luscious' face. She was wondering, how in the hell she was going to pay the rent by herself with Zoe moving out on such short notice.

"I told Rocko that I wasn't leaving you to pay the rent on your own like that. So, he paid it up until the lease runs out in June. That way you'd have time to get a new roommate or find a new crib."

She handed the money-order over to Luscious.

"*And* ... it's isn't just my half. It's the entire rent for each month until the lease ends."

Luscious sat the money-order down beside her on the chair and got up and hugged her friend. She fought back the tears that stung at her eyes. Zoe was such a good friend. She always thought about others. People like her were so rare and didn't come around that often. She understood why Rocko wanted to make her officially his.

"Tell Rocko I said thank you," she sniffled and laughed at the same time. "And tell him I didn't miss the fact that he already filled that money order out to the leasing office."

The two friends burst into laughter.

"He said he wanted to make sure it was paid," Zoe admitted, still laughing.

Luscious sat back down and picked up the money order.

"Na, tell him, I really do thank him," still slightly emotional by the gesture.

Growing up, Luscious always felt overlooked. Although she came from a large family, they weren't close. Everyone was out for themselves, including her mother. Born and raised in poverty, most of her siblings were still trapped in it. Since Luscious made the most money stripping, she was often the person everyone tried to rely on financially. It was rare that anyone thought of her or her needs. Meeting someone like Zoe was a breath of fresh air. It was rare to find people that gave more than they took.

The girls sat and chat for a little while longer. For some reason, there was an eerie vibe that lingered in the air. They knew that things were going to change. Things were going to be vastly different very soon. Not just with their relationship, but with life in general. They just didn't know exactly how yet. They chose not to speak on it; instead, they sat, talked, and laughed like old times. Each one enjoying every second with each other before that unknown change took place. Before they knew it, it was bedtime for Zoe. She had class in the morning and wanted to get at least a few hours of sleep. Retiring to her room, plopped in bed, and called it a night, while Luscious continued to sit in the living room, deep in thought. She had to figure out her next move.

## ❧ 10 ❧

Z oe gave the clerk the twenty-dollar bill Rocko had given to her and used it to pay for their gas. He had picked her up after class and they were in route to enjoy a late lunch. As usual, Rocko was riding around with an empty tank of gas. Zoe could never understand it. He rolled around in a hundred-thousand-dollar G-Wagon but didn't keep gas in it. It was the most ridiculous thing she'd ever seen.

After politely thanking the clerk, Zoe spun around to leave. Much to her dismay, she was met with a familiar face. One that she hadn't seen in a while, *and* one that she could go without seeing for the rest of her life if she had it her way. It was her mother.

Many nights, Zoe dreamed that she would eventually run into Nora. She had practiced what she would say ... What she would do. Tell her how much she despised her, and how much of a piece of shit she was.

She'd been so angry, so hurt, and so broken — but now ... she was no longer any of those things. For the most part, she was at peace. She pitied her mother. Pitied her thought process, as well as her outlook on life. Zoe didn't want revenge; Nora was already suffering.

People constantly talked in the small city outside of Birmingham, and news traveled lightning fast. Zoe had heard how her mother was living. She was working in housekeeping, still partying, and still screwing any nigga that she thought had a couple dollars. Unfortunately for Nora, there wasn't many of them to choose from. Nobody wanted a washed-up woman in her forties who didn't want anything out of life except someone to take care of her. Nora's life was her karma, and it would be that until the day she died.

"Excuse me," Zoe said as she brushed shoulders to move around her mother since she was standing directly in her way.

"Oh, you don't got shit to say to me?" Nora asked, as in disbelief.

She couldn't believe that Zoe would act like she didn't even know her, especially after the shit she'd done.

"No, actually, I don't," Zoe replied calmly as she walked past her mother and went out the door.

Zoe wasn't surprised when Nora stormed behind her boldly to follow her. She had expected Nora to fly hot. She'd always been confrontational. Even as a young girl, she would fight at the drop of a dime.

"Bitch, you better stop when I'm motherfucking talking to you!" Nora yelled with her face tight and her eyes narrowing to slits.

She snatched the back of Zoe's shirt and spun her around to face her.

Zoe snatched back angrily out of reflex. She tossed her purse to the ground and got ready to rumble. Mother or not, things had changed. Today she planned to draw the line. Today, she would let it be known to the woman in front of her, that the abuse ended the day she walked out of the hellhole she once called home.

"Don't you ever fuckin' touch me again!" Zoe growled, as a gust of unexpected rage swept through her.

"Oh, you think you bad, bitch? Come on?" Nora urged her.

She dared her. She planned to beat shit down her legs. She'd never witnessed Zoe with that amount of boldness or animosity towards her. She had no clue what had gotten into her only child, but she had no problem getting it out of her.

"Naaa. I don't think I'm bad," Zoe replied, her body trembling and her lips quivering while she did her best to control her anger.

She took a deep breath before responding to her mother.

"I think you're fuckin' delusional. To think you can run up on me like I owe you something. I don't owe you shit!" she spat, while staring Nora down. "Naaaa ... I don't owe you nothing at all. And I definitely don't owe you, or anyone else a mother-fucking apology if that's what you think you're fuckin' entitled to!"

Nora paused for a minute. She'd never seen her daughter like this. Zoe had always been so meek, so respectful. Zoe had so much anger and frustration pent up inside of her, she felt like she would burst. Her teeth were clenched; her jaws were tight; her head was hurting, and it felt like her heart was going to pound out of her chest.

*You want the truth! You can't handle the fuckin' truth! But here it is anyway bitch!* Zoe thought, before pouring her angry heart out.

"That nigga you beat my ass over and threw me out for — raped me weekly! *Weekly!*" she reiterated for emphasis.

"Whenever he felt like it! If he wanted pussy, I gave it to him! When he wanted his dick sucked — I did it! Not because I wanted to! Or because I wanted to cross you or hurt you! I did it because I didn't have a choice. I did it so I could keep a roof over my head and get through school. I did it because I knew that my weak ass mother would never choose me over the nigga that took care of her!" Zoe screamed in contempt.

Tears flooded her eyes from the painful memories. Zoe hated what she came from — who she came from. But she refused to let her past define her.

"You hated me ... And my whole life I never understood why.

70

Why wouldn't a mother love her own child?" she asked, her lip trembling.

Salty tears slipped down her face revealing the pain she had bottled up inside. The pain ... that had turned into fury.

"I knew I couldn't come to you and tell you anything, because I knew you wouldn't care. I knew that you would never give up your meal ticket for me. You were too concerned with being a bad bitch, instead of being a mother. So, if I owe you anything, it's nothing more than the explanation I just gave you."

The words cut through Nora, leaving her literally speechless. She had no idea. Nora's mind was still stuck in time. Still stuck in a juvenile mentality. She was a grown woman that still thought like a teenager. That childish assumption that everyone was jealous of her. Everyone was hating on her. That the goal was to get a man to take care of her because she was a "bad bitch."

Before Nora could respond, Zoe scooped up her purse and started to walk off. She'd only taken a few steps when she turned around.

"Oh, and just so you know, I've been blessed beyond belief. *He sees everything.*"

Her grandmother used to always tell her that. That there was no escaping the eyes of God. He knew what she had been through and that was all that mattered. God knew why she had made every choice she had made despite how wrong and impure she felt when she made them.

*He sees everything.* The statement was the final words Zoe said to her mother before she turned around, walked off and jumped back into Rocko's truck. She could have said more. She could have told her mother that she was in a relationship where she was loved, respected, and appreciated. She could have rubbed it all in her face, but she didn't need to. Her mother's pain wasn't what she needed to feel better. She had what she needed: love. Not only did she have the most important form of love — self-love; she had Rocko's.

⚜

"YOU OKAY?" ROCKO ASKED TENDERLY AFTER HE HAD PUMPED the gas and got back in the truck.

He had witnessed the argument with the unknown woman who he assumed to be her mother. He figured it was safe to assume since the woman who was also breathtakingly beautiful, bore strikingly similar features to Zoe. Now that she was back in the car, Zoe sat deathly quiet in the driver's seat. She stared out the window and wept silently. Her tear-streamed face buried in the corner so Rocko couldn't see.

In response, Zoe nodded her head yes but didn't speak. She didn't want Rocko to see her in such a weak state. She'd told him only bits and pieces about her mother. That their relationship was rocky, but she had never told him the full story. Although Zoe had been honest about some of the abuse, Rocko had no clue of all that she endured at the hands of her mother and while in her care.

"Zoe, baby look at me," Rocko called to her when he realized there were slim chances of her opening up fully to him.

He took her arm gently and pulled her towards him so she could face him.

"Why you hiding?" he asked.

This time, Zoe didn't fight his attempt to be there for her. When he turned her to face him, she grabbed him and held on to him. She buried her head and his chest and wept openly.

"I hate her," she sniffled. "But I love her too."

"Talk about it," he urged.

He rocked Zoe in his arms, rubbed her back, and kissed the sides of her face. His heart ached for her.

"I hate her because of how she treated me. All she had to do was be a mom. Love me like a normal mom would love her child. Since I was a little girl, all I've known from her was hate. To be a child and feel unwanted. To feel like you're a burden. To feel unwelcome. My whole life I tried to stay out the way, but it was never enough. The only person I had was my grandmother. She did her best to overcompensate for the woman she'd birthed. When she died, that was it. All my joy --- gone. Nothing to look forward to. No one that looked forward to seeing me. No one to hug me. No one to kiss me. Just ... no one. She beat me. She'd berate me. She neglected me. She made my life a living Hell ... But I can't help but still love her."

Zoe shook her head and forced the rest of her tears out. Rocko sat silently and held her. He said nothing. He just wanted her to get it all out before he spoke.

"I – I --- I'm sorry," Zoe stammered with embarrassment.

She hated that she'd allowed herself to be that vulnerable in front of Rocko. She didn't want him thinking she was some mentally ill chick with baggage. She pulled away and glanced up at him bashfully. Lowering her eyes, she avoided contact with his. She wondered what he thought about her now.

"There's no need to be sorry. You needed to let that out. You have every right to express how you feel. I'd never judge you for that. My love for you doesn't change and it damn sure isn't dictated by your past. I do want to be clear about some things going forward though Zoe," Rocko said, his demeanor growing suddenly stern.

Blinking away her tears, Zoe looked to him and noticed the firm expression on his face.

"I want you to open up to me and be honest. Whatever battles you're fighting ... don't have to be fought alone. There's nothing I wouldn't do for you. Nothing I wouldn't give you. There is no problem you should have to face on your own. If I can fix it, I will. But I need you to let me. Let me be there for you. Let me love you. And all I ask in return is that you return that love."

He stared at her intently and lovingly. He meant every word.

"If you need a hug, I'm here. If you need a kiss, I'm here. *I* look forward to seeing you," he emphasized. "I want you to look forward to being with me. I want you to know that you are special. You are important. And you mean a whole lot to someone. That someone is me. Don't you ever forget that. I know it's hard to forget your past, so I won't say that, but I do want you to take joy in the present. Life is about perception. As fucked up as it may sound ... maybe you went through all that bullshit because of the life that awaits you. There is light for you at the end of the tunnel. Find joy in that."

Rocko paused for a moment and then finally continued.

"I'm gon take care of you. You're going to have a good ass life, and I'm going to cheer you on. When you graduate from school. In everything you want to do. I'm proud of you and you are *not* alone. You won't ever be again. Physically or mentally. You heard me?" he asked.

Her lips quivering from emotion, Zoe nodded.

"Yeah," she said finally, choking back sobs. "Thank you, baby," she said.

She wondered where this man was sent from. She leaned in and hugged him some more. While she rested her head into his chest, she worried. She loved him so much it scared her. She prayed he didn't let her down.

LATER THAT NIGHT, ZOE WALKED THROUGH HER MAN'S kitchen, searching for items to prepare dinner. The kitchen was exceptionally small, especially considering the hefty amount he paid monthly for rent. However, the breathtaking river-view from the tenth floor, made the place worth every penny.

"Babe, where is the spatula!" Zoe called out to Rocko, who was in the living room, hanging off the sofa watching the sports channel.

"The what?" Rocko called back out to her.

"The spatula!" she replied.

She didn't understand why he hadn't heard her the first time since he wasn't far. The apartment had an open floor plan, so it wasn't like there were any walls separating them. She guessed he had selective hearing.

"It's in one of those drawers in the island."

After shuffling around in each of the drawers in the island that sat smack dab in the middle of the kitchen, Zoe finally found a black spatula. She shook her head in dismay. It wasn't even one of the metal ones. A cheap-ass plastic spatula. It was bent, peeling, and had clearly seen better days. She made a mental note to trash it once she was done dinner. She hurried back over to the grilled cheese sandwiches she had heating in the skillet and flipped them over. Luckily, they hadn't burned while she was searching for that beat-up ass spatula.

"Here you go babe," Zoe said to Rocko once she was done cooking.

He sat up from his dangling position and took the plate.

"Mmmmm," he smiled. "How you know I fucks with the grilled-cheese?" he asked before taking a gigantic bite from one of the two on the plate.

Zoe giggled at his blatant display of appreciation for the most basic-ass meal ever.

"I didn't. I just hoped and prayed you did, since that's one of the only three things I can make."

"Well you did good babe," he assured her.

Rocko wasn't picky. He didn't care what he ate. As long as he ate. With a mouth full of food and still in mid-chew, he leaned over and gave her a loud, dramatic kiss on the cheek.

"Oh! I forgot. I got a surprise for you," he said, jumping up from where he was seated.

"What is it?" Zoe asked.

She climbed up on the large sofa to sit next to the spot he had just moved from. Rocko didn't respond right away. He stole another bite from his sandwich and slid the plate on the coffee table before running off into his bedroom. When he returned, he stood in front of her and admired her briefly. She was so simple, yet so stunning. Fresh-faced with a messy ponytail, she sat quietly on the sofa with her legs and bare feet pulled underneath of her, wearing nothing but his black t-shirt. She was so oblivious to the beauty she possessed. Completely unaware of the peaceful aura she brought to his world. He loved her so much and he couldn't help but show her every chance he could.

Zoe noticed that when Rocko returned, he was holding two plain, white envelopes. He handed her the first one. She looked at him with curiosity, stared at what he had just given her, and hesitated for a moment.

"Open it," he encouraged.

She slowly tore away the top and pulled out the paper inside. It was a receipt. A massive smile crept along Rocko's face.

"What is it?" he asked her, while faking surprise.

Zoe gasped when she saw what it was. She then sat quietly. She had to let what he'd done sink in. After a few seconds, she finally responded.

"It's a receipt for my tuition."

"Yep. I paid off your last three semesters. Now all you gotta do is take that ass to class. You don't gotta worry about no tuition, no books, no nothing," he said in satisfaction.

Zoe was at a loss for words. She shook her head and blinked her eyes but then stopped. She decided to just let the tears fall. She hated being a cry-baby, *but* he did say she was free to be herself around him. This is who she was. She was vulnerable, she was sensitive, and she was emotional when someone went out of their way to do something extraordinary for her.

"I take it, those are happy tears," he laughed. "Here."

He handed her the other envelope.

Zoe wondered what it could be. The envelope was thick and fat. She sniffled lightly but continued to tear it open. This time though, instead of being a receipt, it was cold-hard-cash.

"Baby, what's this for?" she asked confused.

"That's your allowance. $3k."

"But why?" she stammered in pure disbelief.

They had agreed she would get a job.

"So, you won't feel any pressure. So, you can relax and let the only worries you have, be your education. I asked you to give up running. The least I could do was meet you halfway."

"Babe ... This is more than half-way. This is too much," she admitted.

He stopped her.

"Trust me, baby. It isn't. I make a lot of money. I live well under my means. I can afford to give you more than that. I don't feel the need to though. You're very simple. Very down to earth. Exactly what I want. Everything my folks would want for me. Everything they've prayed about for me. So, take it. Let me take care of you. For once, let yourself receive the love and care you deserve."

Zoe forced a hard swallow down her throat. She was at a loss for words. God sure had a way of doing things. Two years back she would never imagine that she would be the girlfriend of a rich nigga. A rich nigga that adored the hell out of her.

"That's your allowance. You'll get that every week. You can do whatever you want with it. Save it, whatever. I wanted you to understand this relationship is not about control. It's about love. I'm going to give you everything you need so you can still feel in control. That 12k a month you're going to be getting, gives you the freedom to be able to leave whenever you want. Whenever you feel that I no longer make you happy. You get to walk away financially secure. No tuition payments being hung over your head. None of that extra shit. Paid off upfront with your best interest primary. I love you, baby. I just want to make you happy. Take care of you."

Zoe didn't respond. Once again, she was at a loss for words. He had said everything she needed to hear and had dispelled every doubt she had about being with him. Committing to him. She knew God worked in mysterious ways. She knew He was intentional in his timing and gifts. Rocko was her gift from God, and somehow, she would be his. She vowed that she would be of whatever service He had called her for.

Zoe sat down her envelopes and stood up. She hugged Rocko tightly before giving him a passionate kiss.

NORA SAT IN THE MIDDLE OF HER SMALL KITCHEN AT A CARD-table she used for meals. Tonight, instead of eating, she was drinking. She lifted a bottle of Tito's to her lips and threw some of the smooth Vodka into her mouth. She wasn't exactly sure why she was upset. She couldn't quite put her finger on it. She just wanted to hurry up and numb it. Nora wasn't big on facing her demons. She'd rather simply ignore them. She'd been doing just that for the last year; however, seeing Zoe was a painful reminder of how shitty her life was. She was also a painful reminder that no matter how much she tried to forget about her demons, they were still there.

Nora had just turned thirty-four a few weeks ago. She had no man, no money, and a job she hated but couldn't quit. She had no sense of purpose and certainly, nothing worth living for. She wished she had the guts to end her life, but she didn't. She instead would continue to focus on getting by and doing what-ever she could to make herself happy. That was growing harder and harder, especially now that she no longer had a man, nor materials validating her worth. She contemplated going back to Redz and begging him to take her back. She regretted making such a big stink about him screwing her only child. It had made her life a mess. What she regretted the most was even catching them. Life would have been so much easier had she never even known.

When she initially walked in on the two of them, she figured it had to be consensual. However, after honestly thinking about it, she knew it couldn't be. Zoe wasn't raised to do those things. She had been raised to be obedient. She'd always done as she was told and never spoke back. She was humble, modest, and respectful. That's the way her mother had raised her. The same way she'd raised Nora. *Do as you're told and don't talk back.*

Nora had grown up with those same beliefs. Unfortunately, those beliefs would come back to haunt them all when Nora did just that. She would do as she was told and didn't say a word when her mother's husband Rob was raping her on a weekly basis. It was only when Nora became pregnant with Zoe that her mother realized that her man was tiptoeing into her very own daughters' room.

Brought up with strong Christian beliefs, her mother Paula refused to allow Nora to have an abortion. She didn't want law enforcement or Child Services snooping around. Forced to care for a baby she never wanted, Nora would eventually rebel and seek refuge in the streets. Paula would eventually step in and raise Zoe as her own, doing her best to right her wrongs in the process. She had left Rob and tried repeatedly to make amends with Nora. However, it was to no avail.

When Paula passed unexpectedly from a heart attack, Nora would be forced to care for Zoe once again. With a special hatred for the child, she couldn't help but mistreat her. Her conception had been evil and forced, so Nora treated her accordingly. In her eyes, she was the real victim. Forced out of her innocence. Forced to not only birth a child, but also care for a child that she did not want. It bothered her even more seeing Zoe all grown up. Riding around in a fancy truck, with her rich, probably drug-dealer boyfriend by her side. It wasn't fair.

Zoe's birth had done nothing but ruin her life. It had made her bitter. Made her resentful. She was only fourteen years old when she had her. From fourteen to eighteen she had to deal with everyone in the town slandering her name and whispering about the origins of the baby she had out of wedlock at such a tender age. Out of embarrassment, Paula had sworn her to secrecy about the identity of Zoe's father. Instead, assisting in tarnishing the reputation of her only child. The damage had a lasting impact on Nora ... and it showed.

## ❧ 11 ❧

Niko sat on the phone and listened to one of his babies-mamas argue about their son's tuition not being paid.

"I told you it was a mistake, damn!" He let out an exasperated grunt.

"Yeah, I bet it was nigga! Funny how you can remember to keep your new bitch laced, but you can't remember to pay your son's fuckin' tuition!" his baby mama roared into the phone.

"It's gonna get paid. I'll bring you the money later."

Before he could say another word, she hung up in his ear. Out of all three of his baby-mamas, she was the biggest pain in the ass. He only had one kid by her, but it was always some bullshit every time she called. Always worried about what he did for the next person. A typical, hating ass hoe.

Niko had four children by three different women. In his opinion, each one of them trapped him. They were all money-hungry, strippers or ex-strippers. Being the boss-ass-nigga that he was, he would often frequent strip-clubs. Not just for leisure, but also for business purposes. Because of this, he mingled and smashed strippers regularly. Once they saw what type of cash he had and threw around on a regular basis, all the stripper bitches were on his top, eager to get a piece.

He knew for a fact they weren't interested in genuinely. It certainly wasn't because of his dashing good looks or personality. In fact, he had grown up being teased daily by niggas and bitches alike. His whole life he'd been called fat and unruly --- Even by family. It also didn't help that he wasn't the most well-behaved child coming up. He had a quick temper and his attitude was downright horrible. His whole life, he was poorly received. For that reason, he didn't fuck with too many people; only a select few, with Rocko being one of them. The two men had been raised together by their grandmother, growing up like brothers, in a religious household. Since he was younger, Rocko was the good child and he was the bad child. To put it simply, they were opposites. While he himself was a promiscuous party-animal, who really didn't give a damn about most people, Rocko was studious, reserved, and quiet. The lady's loved him, but he was old-school --- very traditional. Rocko didn't date often, and when he did, he put his all into it.

Niko tossed his phone in his seat and massaged his temples in frustration. The saying was true: *mo' money, mo' problems.* His latest one was Luscious. She had just informed him that she was pregnant. It certainly wasn't the news he wanted to hear. With four children, it wouldn't have been such a huge issue to add one more with another stripper. The problem was he was no longer a single man and couldn't just be popping up with a brand-new baby that wasn't conceived with his wife. All his children were conceived before he was married a year ago. There was no way that he could let an outside pregnancy get back to his wife. Not only was she his partner, but she was also the lifeline to his business.

Despite how he tried to explain that to Luscious, she didn't seem to understand. In fact, none of the conversations that they had went well. The last one, he told her flat out he didn't want the baby. In response, she flew hot and expressed to him how she intended to end their sexual relationship. Not that he cared one way or the other. She could disappear off the face of the Earth today or tomorrow and he wouldn't give a damn. Besides, she would soon be of little use come soon. He'd just been informed that their business relationship was going to be ending because of his love-struck ass cousin Rocko. His cousin already knew the policy that the runners come in teams. By snatching Zoe off the route, Luscious was all alone, and that was a no go.

Ever since Rocko had been kicking it with Zoe, he'd become head over hills. But ... that's how his cousin was. If he was passionate about something, he put his all in it. If he loved someone, he put his all in them. Although Niko wanted to advise Rocko against it, he didn't. He couldn't blame him. Zoe did seem like a keeper. Not only was she gorgeous but she was in college. That was right up Rocko's alley. Her most obvious flaw was that she used to be a stripper. He personally would never even think of putting his all into a broad that stripped. He certainly wouldn't wife her and make her his girlfriend. However, he wanted his cousin to be happy and that's exactly what he seemed to be. Unfortunately for Niko, that newfound happiness was fuckin' up business.

It wasn't much he could do besides accept things for what they were. Honestly, it would be like the pot calling the kettle black. Niko smashed their runners all the time. Even gone as far and had babies by them. How could he tell his cousin anything? So here he was ... back to square one and looking for new cash-strapped fools to run his drugs from city to city. And he needed them soon. He didn't have time to look for two new ones. He had a couple of people in mind; however, he knew that using them was going to start some drama. Unfortunately, it didn't look like he had much of a choice. He was on his way to meet the two of them now. He hoped it worked out.

&#10086;&#10086;&#10086;

LUSCIOUS HAD BEEN SICK ALL MORNING BUT SHE STILL GOT dressed and hit the road for her last run. She was still partly emotional because of the way Niko had acted when she told him she was pregnant. She didn't even know why she was so upset since truthfully; she was completely expecting the reaction of him not wanting the baby. What she didn't expect was for him to be so cold towards her. Despite being upset, she knew she couldn't let her anger and hurt consume her. She had to be focused so she could get her last run done.

Since she was in her feelings, she set her auto play to R&B once she got into her car. Surprisingly one of her favorite songs by Tink starting blaring through the speakers of the compact car.

*Is that too muchhhhhh? Cuz, I've been on a search and I'm losing my hope. Is that too much? Is that too muchhhh? Trying to find a love in a world so coldddd.*

The song couldn't have had better timing. It wasn't that Luscious was necessarily looking for someone to love her, but ... it would be nice. Just like Zoe, she'd also come from a loveless home. Middle child and the only girl of five children born to a single mother, Luscious grew up forced to be tough at an early age. Her mother seemed to spit babies out like sunflower seeds; however, she lacked tremendously on the nurturing part.

A part of Luscious wanted her baby. A child's love was unconditional and without expectations. However, the last thing she wanted to do was bring a baby into the world lacking the love from their father. She knew how it felt to grow up without a dad. She didn't want that for her child.

With or without Niko's support, she was leaning towards keeping the baby. She had been calling Niko to explain to him that she'd love his support; however even if he didn't want to be a part of the child's life, she was still having it. As Tink continued to croon through the speakers, Luscious couldn't shake the urge to call Niko again.

"Siri, call Niko," she said loudly.

"*Calling Niko,*" Siri responded before the call connected and started to ring.

"What?" Niko replied impatiently, answering on the fourth ring.

He sounded not only frustrated by her call, but also occupied. Luscious could hear music blaring in the back and several different female voices talking. As she listened more closely, the voices sounded too familiar.

"Is this a bad time?" Luscious asked.

"What?" Niko replied irritably. "I'm taking care of business like I always do. Wassup?"

"Niko. You already know what we need to talk more about."

"Man, I'm not about to get into it with you this early in the day about that. I already told you that now isn't a good time for me to be having no more babies. I'm cool on that. You gotta get rid of it."

Luscious paused for a moment but then finally replied.

"Niko, I decided I'm keeping it. You don' have to be in my baby's life but you are going to help me take care of it financially."

"Why the fuck do I have to help you with shit if you know I'm not with it!" he snapped. "Will y'all shut the fuck up. I'm on the phone!" he yelled at the people in the background.

"Damn nigga, you don't gotta be acting all funky," one of the unknown females replied sharply in the background.

Luscious immediately recognized the voice this time. She immediately thought back to when the call first started and how there were two women talking. She now knew exactly who he was with. She couldn't believe the audacity of his ass.

"Niko, what the fuck are you doing with Smoke and Toots?" she demanded to know.

Luscious did her best to concentrate on the road as she felt her anger level soar. Niko never ceased to amaze her. One minute he was fucking her and the next minute he was with Smoke and Toots.

"Man, I don't gotta answer to you. You not my woman," he countered.

"Nigga fuck you! I see now yo' ass for everybody. Cola wasn't enough. You gotta fuck with those dick eating, ass bitches too!" she screamed, leaning forward, and slamming her hand against the dashboard.

"Bitch, you need to calm the fuck down. Don't worry about what I do. The only thing you need to worry about is handling that situation."

Before Luscious had a chance to reply, the call was disconnected. She tried dialing him again several times. However, he repeatedly hit ignore, she knew he wasn't going to answer. This was what he did every single time they got into it. He would hang up and then ignore her calls.

A flood of emotions swept through her body. As much as she hated to cry, she couldn't help it. She'd held in her cries long enough, and she finally decided to let them out. An army of tears flowed down her face as she balled her eyes out. She was tired of crossing rivers for people who wouldn't even jump over a puddle for her. She had done everything Niko asked of her.

Fucking with him, she'd lost her lifeline: her job. It wasn't much but it was something she could always fall back on. Something that had helped provide her with a comfortable life. Now that the club was gone, she had zero streams of income. Pregnant and no longer able to transport because she didn't have a partner, she was now in a bind. She doubted that Niko would still let her run for him even if she had a partner or not. She'd done nothing but look out for Niko and be the ride or die chick that he claimed he needed. It hadn't gotten her anywhere.

Luscious thought about all the times she came through for Niko. She didn't talk to the police when they came asking about the club shooting, and she'd even agreed to run drugs up and down I-83 for his ass. Despite consistently displaying her loyalty, he still decided to shit on her. Luscious felt heartbroken and betrayed, and no matter how hard she tried to tell herself that it would be okay, she didn't feel that way.

Luscious did her best to blink away tears while she gripped

the steering wheel and raced down the highway toward Atlanta. Feeling her nose drip profusely from the snot that usually accompanied her tears, she lifted and dug through her console to see if she could find any loose tissues. Not seeing any, she leaned down and pulled open her glove box.

*I knew I had a few somewhere*, she thought to herself when she spotted a small stack of brown Wendy's napkins. She reached back down to dig them out.

It seemed like she had only taken her eyes off the road two seconds; however, when she looked back up, traffic had slowed to a near halt because of construction. She hadn't even noticed the orange construction signs several miles back because she was too busy crying and arguing with Niko.

Luscious mashed her foot down on the break as she noticed the car in front of her seemed to have stopped moving. Unfortunately, she wasn't quick enough. She swerved to the right to avoid rear-ending the car in front of her, but because she was in the far-left lane, she still was headed right into the side of another vehicle. Her heart racing in her chest, Luscious squeezed her eyes tight before she felt her car collide violently into another.

"MS. BAILEY?" THE NURSE CALLED. THE AIR CONDITIONING was running high and all the monitors and machines going caused her to speak up. She wasn't sure if her patient had heard her.

"Ms. Bailey," the nurse repeated, this time louder.

Luscious' eyes were heavy, but when she heard her name being called, she still managed to flutter them until she eventually opened them. Her eyes began searching for the voice that called her. It had been a long time since anyone had called her by her first or last name. She leaned her head in the direction of the voice.

"Ms. Bailey. Glad to see you're awake. How you feeling?" the woman in a tan set of nursing scrubs asked.

An older black lady with salt and pepper hair, she wore a thick pair of glasses and had a stethoscope dangling from her neck.

"I feel a little groggy," she admitted.

Luscious paused and scanned the small room she was in. She didn't have to ask where she was; she already knew. She was in the hospital. Which one she was unsure of. She had been in a car accident. That part she remembered. She glanced down at her arms and legs. She didn't seem too injured. But then it hit her. *Shit*, she thought to herself, once the details began to flood her mind. She was on a run. She wrecked the car with all the drugs in it. *Fuck!* Then she also remembered that she was pregnant.

"My baby," she cried out.

"Your baby is just fine. The moment you came in and we got your blood work back we were able to determine that you were pregnant. We've checked you several times and ran all the tests to ensure your baby is doing perfectly fine. Heart rate is good. Everything is okay," she assured Luscious.

Unfortunately for Luscious, that was only just one of her problems.

"You came in unconscious and were a little banged up but thankfully it was all minor. You're living so that's a blessing," the nurse smiled. She moved from the other side of the room and walked closer to Luscious' bedside so she could explain what was going on.

"From what EMT told us, your car was pretty banged up. You're very lucky young lady.

That statement was debatable. Luscious wasn't sure if she really were. With all the drugs that she was transporting, she couldn't quite make that determination yet.

"We have you on some pain meds, but you should be fine without them."

"Can I leave?" Luscious asked, cutting her off. She knew the nurse meant well but she was eager to get out of there and as far away as she could. Panic was setting in as Luscious realized the gravity of what was going on. What *could* happen if they found the drugs in her now banged up rental? She had no idea if they'd even found them yet, but if they did, she wanted to be long gone.

"I need to get out of here. I feel fine. Can I leave please?" Luscious asked again.

The nurse hesitated and then turned and gave Luscious a somber look.

"Well ... that's not up to me, sweetie. You have a couple of nice police officers out here that are going to need to ask you some questions."

"Fuck," she muttered, her stomach growing heavy.

Luscious scanned the room. There was only one window, and it appeared as if she were on at least the fourth floor. With all those kilos she had in her trunk, she had the urge to make a run for it. Her heart sank to her feet when she realized what was about to happen. Remorse and regret began to consume her. How could she let her emotions consume her and cause her to have an accident?

*Shit, shit, shit,* she thought. *I'm fucked.*

"You rest as best as you can, sweetheart. I'm going to go head out."

Luscious sighed and threw her head back into the pillow she lay against. She felt the tears forming in her eyes. Before they could slip down her face, she heard the door open. In walked the Feds.

## ❧ 12 ❧

"You coming in?" Rocko asked Zoe while she sat in the passenger seat unusually quiet.

Zoe had just gotten out of class and since her car needed some brake work, Rocko had picked her up to take her home. While in route, he got a call from Niko. Since this was Zoe and Luscious' last week doing runs for them, Niko placed the utmost urgency on them finding their replacements. Being partly at fault for their sudden departure, Rocko didn't complain when Niko asked him to stop what he was doing so they could meet the two females he had had hand-picked as replacements.

He had just pulled into the parking lot of the club that Niko told him to meet him at. Since he didn't know how long he was going to be, he figured he would invite Zoe in so she could grab a bite to eat or something to drink while he handled business.

"Na, I'm not coming in," Zoe finally responded, swallowing the huge lump that had formed in her throat. "I'm just gonna wait in the car," she said, before peering around nervously.

Noticing her sudden shift in mood, Rocko asked her, "You okay?"

"Yeah, I'm fine. Just ready to get home. Got a little

headache," she admitted, although that was only half of the real problem.

Zoe lightly pressed her hand against her forehead for emphasis.

"Hurry up ok?" she asked him before leaning in towards him and giving him a light kiss. She wanted to reassure him that she was fine, although that was far from the truth.

"Aight. I'll do my best," he promised, before jumping out and slamming the door closed.

As soon as Zoe saw Rocko disappear in the doors of the building, she let out a nervous sigh of relief. He had literally brought her into the parking lot of her tormentor. It was The Sugar House's number one competitor: Club Heat. The strip club owned and operated by none other than her mother's ex-boyfriend Redz.

❦

"WHAT'S UP. SORRY, I'M RUNNING A LITTLE LATE," ROCKO said before joining Niko and the two young women accompanying him at the booth.

"It's all good baby," Niko said. "You know I can't get started without my right-hand," he admitted.

"Ladies, this is my partner Rocko. Rocko, this is Smoke and Toots."

The two women smiled seductively at Rocko, admiring his good lucks and manners. They wondered why Cola never mentioned that Niko had a fine ass partner. But then again, they didn't blame her. They never did anything in complete honesty.

Peeping their shady-like behavior from the moment he began dealing with Cola, Niko figured he would use it to his advantage. It wasn't unusual for strippers and hood-bitches to fuck on the same nigga. Noticing their extra friendly grins, extended eye-contact, and flirty behavior and dialogue on multiple occasions, Niko didn't hesitate to get with them when the opportunity presented itself. Not only had he fucked Smoke and Toots behind Cola's back, he had even fucked them together. They were on board with whatever he presented, as long as he blessed them with dead presidents. To them, it was more money than they'd ever received from a nigga; to him, it was merely chump change.

With Cola's erratic, ridiculous behavior causing the club to close, they'd become especially resentful. The closest profitable strip-club was nearly forty-minutes away. Not only was that too far for their liking, there was also far too much competition in the city for the small selection of clubs. She had fucked their money up big time and they were diligently searching for any hustle that would keep their pockets fat.

After leaving The Sugar House, the best option they had was to work for Redz at Club Heat. The girls hated working for Redz. Not only was he a crook, he was a perverted crook. He overcharged all that girls that worked for him and he also regularly forced them to perform sexual acts on him for free. That's why when Niko came to them with a business opportunity, they didn't hesitate to take him up on his offer. They sat quietly while Rocko's fine ass ran over the details to their next move. The more he talked, the better it got. The shit he was kicking, was right up their alley.

*THE FUCK IS TAKING THIS NIGGA SO LONG?* ZOE WONDERED AS she glanced down at her phone for what felt like the 10<sup>th</sup> time. Rocko had been in the building for nearly thirty-minutes. She tapped her foot nervously and stared out the window and into the parking lot, as a mixture of nervousness and irritation consumed her. Before she could glance down at her phone again, the abrupt and obnoxious chime from the default ringtone, caused her to jump. She looked down and didn't recognize the number. Out of boredom, she answered it anyway.

"Zoe," Luscious cried into the phone.

Her voice was grief-laden and shaky. Zoe could tell instantly that something was wrong.

"Luscious, what's wrong?" she asked.

She gripped her phone tightly against her ear and waited for her friend's response. A wave of nausea swam over her and produced a sick feeling in the pit of her stomach. She now remembered Luscious' last run was today. She hadn't even called her to make sure she was okay. She had just spoken to Luscious last night and she was upset about her situation with Niko. The feeling of guilt immediately hit her. She should have called and checked on her friend. She probably wasn't in the right mental state to do the run.

Zoe couldn't help the flow of negative thoughts swarming through her head. It was the way Luscious said her name when she picked up. She knew something was wrong.

"Luscious! What's wrong?" she asked again sternly.

Zoe was not only worried, but she was growing impatient. Luscious had paused and she heard people in the background talking to her.

"I uhh uhhh, need you to come get me," she stammered.

Zoe could tell that she was scared. She had always worn her emotions on her sleeve, and this time was no different. Her behavior was starting to put fear in Zoe as well.

"Luscious, what the fuck is going on? Where are you? Who are you with? What the fuck happened."

She rambled off question after question to her friend, only to be met with more brief periods of silence.

"I'll tell you when you get here. Just please, come get me," she cried.

"Okay! Tell me where you are."

Luscious quickly rambled off an address and then made promises to text it to her. Before Zoe could utter another word, Luscious had hung up.

"Fuck!" Zoe muttered aloud angrily.

She had no clue what was going on, but whatever it was, it couldn't be good. She looked at the entrance doors to Club Heat and Rocko was still nowhere in sight. She cursed her luck. She didn't have a choice but to go inside. She needed to tell Rocko they had an emergency and needed to leave.

Zoe had vowed to stay away from Redz the last time she'd seen him, and that also included, anything his ass owned. Her girl needed her though, so, with a big, giant *"fuck it,"* Zoe unlocked the doors and hopped down and out of Rocko's truck. Before she could shut the door to the vehicle, she got another text. It was from Luscious and it read: *Please don't tell Rocko or Niko. Not a word about this until I tell you what's going on.*

Zoe swallowed the rock-hard lump that had instantly formed in her throat and headed into the club. She now had no doubt that whatever had happened ... was bad.

⚜

ZOE ENTERED CLUB HEAT AND AFTER PASSING THE FRONT desk that also served as security, she began her search for Rocko. As Zoe walked, fear cloaked her. She prayed she didn't run into Redz. She didn't want any confrontations. She just wanted to get to wherever Rocko and Niko were and then get the fuck out of there. Walking briskly through the establishment, her eyes darted around nervously for her man. While she looked, she couldn't help but notice how run-down the place had gotten since the last time she'd seen it. She'd been in the building a few times with her mother when she was younger, but each time she distinctly remembered it being in better shape.

"Excuse me miss, can I help you?" one of the employees called out to her.

Zoe waved her off. "No, I'm good. I'm just looking for someone."

She headed to the VIP section. If things were still the same as they were years ago, then the VIP section was still in the back.

Just as she arrived at the back of the club, she spotted Rocko's handsome face. Relief washed over her. However, relief was immediately replaced with anger when she saw two faces she could live without. It was Smoke and Toots. She was instantly annoyed. She knew it was nobody's doing but Niko. After all the shit that happened with Cola, why would he go and recruit her besties Smoke and Toots to work with him? It seemed to Zoe, that Niko was the real problem. Or he was just a real idiot.

"What are you doing?" she asked Rocko as she approached their table that was tucked in the corner.

She wasn't completely sure if Rocko knew what happened at the club the night it got shut down, but she didn't want him hanging around the likes of Smoke and Toots. They fucked and sucked anything. She was surprised one wasn't whispering in Rocko's ear when she walked up. Noticing unusual anger on Zoe's face, Rocko went to reply but Smoke beat him to it.

"Mmmmm. This bitch," Smoke muttered, rolling her eyes. Toots didn't say anything, but Zoe could detect a smirk creeping up in the corners of her mouth.

"Watch your mouth," Rocko demanded, staring her down with fury flickering in his eyes. He didn't normally hit women, but a part of him wanted to smack her out of her seat.

"Na, she ain't gotta watch shit. She gon' know when I beat that ass," Zoe snapped. "What the fuck are you doing in here with these bitches anyway?" she demanded to know.

"We taking care of business Zoe. I told you that."

"Yeah, I bet. Taking care of business with hoes like these. After all the shit that happened at the Sugar House?"

"Ain't nobody finna be too many more of your hoes," Toots finally chimed in.

"Look Zoe, sit down and chill the fuck out," Niko demanded, growing impatient.

Zoe spun her head around to face him. "Nigga you don't check me. I'm not yo' bitch to check."

Zoe glared at Rocko, spun around on her heels, and stormed off.

"Facts nigga. You sho' nuff out of line. Worry about these two. I'll handle my girl," Rocko said to his cousin angrily.

"Please do handle that hoe," Smoke added, while Toots rolled her eyes.

"Niko." Rocko paused and took a deep breath.

He'd had enough of the two smart-mouthed bitches. Niko could never seem to keep any of the bitches in line. How were they going to have order when their runners didn't even respect their authority? Rocko now knew that Niko didn't really have shit under control at all.

"These bitches a dub for me. They don't get my approval."

Rocko got up from the table and walked off.

By the time he got outside, Zoe was gone. He scanned and drove around the parking lot in search of her, but she was nowhere to be found. He even tried calling her phone dozens of times, but she didn't pick up. After a while, her phone began going straight to voicemail.

He didn't understand why she was so upset. He figured it was because of the way Niko had spoken to her. It wasn't cool and Rocko knew that. He'd checked him, but he was going to check him again about it.

Rocko sat and waited in the parking lot, but after about thirty-minutes, and no sign of Niko, he left. Something told him that he was going to try and proceed with the Smoke and Toots despite his disapproval. If he did, Rocko knew what he had to do.

## ❄ 13 ❄

Zoe had cooled down a bit and was now headed to get Luscious. After storming out of Club Heat, she hailed an Uber from her phone and picked up her car. Even though the brakes needed work, it was still safe enough to drive. Zoe was actually a little embarrassed by how she acted. She knew Rocko wouldn't lay down with any chicks like Smoke and Toots; however, she still couldn't help but feel anger and jealous when he saw them talking to them with Niko. They looked like they were on a double date or something. She never wanted to come between him and his business with his cousin. She didn't want to ever interfere with is business ever.

She still couldn't get over the fact that Niko was rude to her in defense of some stank hoes. She personally didn't like him and struggled to see what her girl saw in his fat ass. He wasn't ugly, but he wasn't attractive either.

When Zoe finally pulled up to the address Luscious had sent her, she was surprised that it was the parking lot of a hospital emergency room, way out in Pell City, Alabama. Zoe drove slowly and looked carefully around the parking lot until she spotted Luscious standing outside, nervously smoking a cigarette.

Zoe knew something was up since she hadn't been smoking anything after finding out that she was pregnant. When Luscious spotted Zoe's car drive up, her eyes widened and she quickly mashed her cigarette out against the building. She wasted no time scurrying over to the car and hopping in. She looked around and over her shoulder nervously. Almost as if she were scared that someone was watching or following her.

"What's going on Luscious? Where's the car?" Zoe questioned her before she could even get comfortable in her seat.

Zoe studied Luscious carefully and could tell that she was going through something. *What* was the question. She looked like she'd had a rough day. Her usually long, silky weave was disheveled and tangled at the ends. Her makeup was smeared, and she had a bloody bandage taped to the side of her head.

"I fucked up," she whispered, tears welling up in her eyes.

"What do you mean, you fucked up?" Zoe asked her.

"I fucked up. I wrecked the car. I don't know how ... but I rear-ended someone," she admitted.

"What!" Zoe asked.

She hadn't gotten out of the parking lot yet, so she whipped the car into a space and tried to park. She wanted to make sure she was hearing her friend correctly ... because if she was, then she was in a heap of trouble.

"No! Don't park. Keep going. Drive! Get me as far the fuck away from here as possible."

Zoe reluctantly put the car back in drive and began heading back to Birmingham.

"What did they find?" Zoe asked. She had already found her exit out of the town and had slipped back onto the highway before springing her latest question on her friend. There was no sense in beating around the bush. She needed to know what they were truly up against.

"Everything," Luscious admitted shakily.

Zoe's shoulders fell and her head slumped at the revelation.

"Shit Lush. We're fucked."

"Don't say that Zoe," she cried. She knew she was fucked but she couldn't bear to hear the words.

Zoe looked back over at Luscious and saw the grief and worry in her face. She knew her friend was doing her best to be positive.

"Was it the Feds?"

"Yeah ... I was still in and out when they first brought me in. There were local police on the scene, then in the room. Next thing I know, the uniforms were gone, there was a nurse and then there were plain clothes officers."

"What did they ask you to do?"

"Tell them where it came from and who it came from."

"Did you?"

"No, but I told them that I would. That's the only way that they would let me out."

"Did you sign anything?" Zoe continued to pry.

"Yeah, that was the only way." Luscious buried her head into the palm of her hands and sobbed. "I'm pregnant Zoe. I can't go to jail. I can't go to jail behind a sorry ass nigga like Niko."

"But you knew the risk when we signed up for this shit. We both knew the risks," Zoe reminded her.

"That's easy for you to say when you're not the one under the gun!" she snapped back.

"But now Rocko is! That puts me under the gun too!"

"Fuck Rocko, Zoe! You're my best-friend! My sister! This isn't about him."

Zoe sighed. "You're right. I love you Luscious, and you know I'll go to the end of the world for you, but this isn't just about you, and you know that. If you take the easy way out of this mess, you have to throw someone else under the bus. That's either going to be Niko and Rocko, or both. So, it's about him too. It's about all three of you. Look Luscious, you know I'll always look out for you but ... I gotta look out for Rocko too. I love him and I don't want him to fall behind this shit. Niko on the other hand. Fuck him. But I don't want to Rocko fall, just like I don't want to see you fall. We just gotta figure something out."

With her lips trembling, and tears steady falling, Luscious nodded her head in agreement.

"Zoe, I need you to promise me that you won't say anything to Rocko. If you do, he's going to tell Niko. I want to be the one to tell him. He's gotta hear it from me first."

Zoe shook her head. She hated to agree to something like that. As serious a mess that they were in, they needed to let them know what was going on. It was also going to be hard to hide the fact that there was no car and no delivery. Rocko had been blowing up her phone non-stop. They were going to want some answers when they got back to Birmingham.

"Okay Luscious. But I only can lie for so long. You're coming back with no car *and* no drugs. How are you going to account for being gone all day without communicating with anyone?" she asked. "You can't just go missing in action and don't expect to raise eyebrows."

She looked over at Luscious and she had a vacant look on her face. She didn't have a clue. Zoe sighed in response.

"How much time did they give you?" Zoe asked.

"Twenty-four hours."

*Fuck*, Zoe thought. There was no way that was enough time for Luscious to make a solid decision. There was no way that she was going to be rational. Zoe already had a feeling she knew what Luscious was going to do. Niko wasn't loyal to anyone but his damn self so she couldn't say she blamed her. She just prayed that Luscious hadn't told her too much. That she hadn't ran down all the details of their business. She didn't want Rocko to get caught up or be implicated in any way.

The women rode in silence all the way back to Birmingham. Zoe's mind was hard at work trying to come up with any kind of way that her girl could get out of the message she managed to fall in. Luscious on the other hand was thinking of ways she could skip town undetected. She wasn't built for it and she didn't want to face it.

She knew people that knew people. She could have a whole new identity in a matter of days. The more and more she thought about it, the more she realized that was her only chance.

When they finally arrived back at Luscious' home, Zoe walked her in to ensure she was okay. Understanding everything she'd been through she told her she would be returning to stay the night with her.

"Why don't you take a hot shower, lay down and relax. I'm going to run home and get some clothes and come back and stay the night with you. You're not dealing with this alone."

Luscious agreed and Zoe headed home. She looked at the time on her dashboard and she felt her stomach fall to her feet. It was nearly three in the morning. Her phone was dead, and she hadn't talked to Rocko since she stormed out of Redz club.

*Shit*, she thought to herself. She knew that he was going to be pissed when she pulled up.

*Not as pissed as he's gonna be when he finds out what the fuck is up.*

🪷

It was nearly 4 a.m. when Zoe walked into her apartment. It was dark, but she didn't bother to turn on the lights. She didn't want to wake Rocko. She knew she was going to have to deal with him in the morning, since she had no doubt that he was going to be royally pissed come that time. She hadn't been answering her phone since she'd left the club earlier that day.

She sat her purse down quietly on a stand right next to the door and tip-toed quietly through the house. She just wanted to grab some clothes and leave right back out so she could be there for her girl Luscious. Before she made it to the middle of the open room, the sound of Rocko's deep voice, caused her to jump

"Where the fuck ... have you been?" he asked angrily. The tone and volume of his voice was uncharacteristic of him.

"You scared the shit out of me," she stammered, clutching her pounding chest. "Why the hell are you sitting in the dark?" she asked, stalling for time by intentionally ignoring his question.

"I asked you a question." He got up off the couch and began walking towards her. For a moment, she thought he was going to grab her, but instead, he went and flicked the switch by the door, turning on the light.

He walked over to her and stood directly in her face, his blazing eyes piercing directly into hers. He searched her eyes for any signs of deceit but couldn't seem to find any. Only thing he saw was worry. He hated to question the woman that he had grown to love so fiercely, but things just didn't add up.

"Where were you Zoe?" he asked again, slowing down the pace of his voice for

emphasis. "I called your phone all day after you took off out the club. I searched the parking lot for you and then called you non-stop. We called Luscious all day. First, you go missing in action, and then her. You need to give me some answers."

Zoe's lips quivered. Not because she feared Rocko, but because she didn't want to betray the trust of her friend. She knew how the game went. After everything that went down, Luscious was in danger, and she could be too.

"Please Rocko. I can't say. I don't want to talk about this right now." She went to walk off, but Rocko grabbed her arm and stopped her.

He looked at her and could see the fear and uncertainty in her eyes. *What are you hiding? What are you scared of?* he wondered.

Zoe's eyes darted towards his in shock. "Rocko, take your fucking hands off me," she demanded calmly. He immediately released his grip and cursed himself for losing his temper.

"Look Zoe, I'm sorry but this is serious. You need to hear me when I say," he began explaining. "With Luscious going ghost, it makes everyone think one thing. That some shit went down or that she's up to something foul. I've never doubted your loyalty to me, but I do know that you are going to do what you can to protect your homegirl. But I need you to trust me and tell me what happened. Trust is everything in a business like this. If something happened, tell me so I understand decide the next move. Tell me what happened, so I can try to fix it," he begged her. "But please, baby, don't leave me blind. Tell me. Remember, I told you ---"

"There's no problem I have to face on my own." She finished his sentence, her voice crackling and eyes welling up with tears.

"Right. Don't hold that weight. Let me handle it," he begged.

Salty tears trickled down Zoe's face as she knew she had to do the unthinkable. She had no choice but to confide in her man. Luscious was already in a mess. A mess that they were in no way, shape, or form prepared to handle on their own. This was the downside of the game. She hated to betray her friend; however, the problem that they were faced with was just too large for them to tackle on their own.

"Okay." She let out a deep sigh. You're going to need to sit down for this one," she said, and then proceeded to go over everything Luscious had told her *and* that she suspected.

When Zoe finished briefing Rocko on what was really going on, he was at a loss for words. They were in some deep shit and he had to get up with Niko immediately. They were going to fix it together. They had to, or their whole empire would soon come crumbling down.

"Rocko, you can't tell Niko okay. Luscious promised me not to tell you. You know how Niko is. If you say something to him, he's going to go ballistic. Please let her tell him.

"Okay," he said solemnly.

He hated lying, and he especially hated lying to someone he loved. He had no choice but to inform Niko about what was going on. He just prayed that the situation didn't affect his and Zoe's relationship.

LUSCIOUS HOVERED OVER THE TOILET BOWL AS CLOSELY AS SHE could, so the contents of her stomach could land in it. After feeling like there was nothing more, she got up, rinsed her mouth out and washed her face.

She knew all the stress that she was dealing with was part of the reason she was feeling extra sick. She didn't know if it was morning sickness or sickness caused from the overwhelming sense of dread she was feeling. *This shit can't be good for the baby*, she thought. She stared the mirror and didn't like what she saw. She looked worn --- defeated, and that's exactly how she felt.

She walked quietly back into her room and crawled in her bed. All she wanted to do was sleep. She prayed that she was having a bad nightmare and that she would eventually wake up. She didn't know what she was going to do. The Feds were clear about what they wanted from her. They had asked her who gave her the drugs. Where they were coming from, and where they were going.

Luscious hadn't been completely honest with Zoe. The Feds wanted names. As many names as she could give them. As many locations as she could give them. She'd done her best to stall for time and fake them out, but they weren't going for it. For her to get out of that hospital, she had to give them at least one name, with promises to give them more later.

As much as she hated to even talk to the Feds when they were bombarding her with questions, she didn't have a choice. She'd given them Niko's name. She didn't want them dragging her out of the hospital to some cold interrogation room. She didn't want them to hover over her and question her for hours. She didn't have any lawyer money or any real means to fight a Fed case.

She was so confused it was sickening. A part of her wanted to remain silent and allow Niko to assist her. Possibly foot her legal fees. That option would be best for him. Unfortunately, he wouldn't even answer the damn phone for her. Luscious knew that if she tried to take the method that benefited him most, it would only be a matter of time before he simply changed his number leaving her to fend for herself.

Although she was torn about what to do, she wasn't stupid, and she kept her ears glued to the streets. She'd heard how Niko got down. She'd heard about all the different bitches who'd gone down by taking charges while running for his sorry ass. It wasn't going to be her. She didn't care about no code. She didn't care what she had agreed to. She wasn't going to be his next fool. She had a baby in her belly that she had to protect. Niko was going to take responsibility for his own drugs. He just didn't know it yet. It would be a cold day in hell before she gave her loyalty to someone that didn't give zero fucks about her. That's what she was trying to convince herself anyway.

## ❧ 14 ❧

"He's asleep," the woman murmured into the phone groggily. Through squinted eyes, she glanced down at the phone and read the time. It was 6 a.m.

"I'm sorry to disturb you but I need you to wake him up for me please, Carmen. You know I wouldn't call and wake you out of your sleep and bother you if it weren't important. I need him to get up. I'm on my way over there and I need to talk to him right away."

"Okay," she replied as she got straight up out of her bed and slid her bare feet to the floor.

She slept in the master bedroom, while most nights Niko fell asleep downstairs in the living room. He was usually out late at night, and most of the time he came in drunk. He usually had no energy or desire to take the short walk upstairs and lie in the bed next to his wife.

Carmen and Niko had been married for a little over a year and they'd had more than a few rough rides. The main issue was Niko was dishonest and he was a cheater. Although he gave her whatever her heart desired, the one thing she wanted, he wouldn't give to save his life.

"Niko," Carmen called, out gently before reaching down and shaking him.

He was sprawled out comfortably on their massive wrap-around sectional, snoring lightly.

"Niko," Carmen called again.

This time he stirred slowly, and then his eyes flew open.

"Huh?" he grumbled.

Carmen rolled her eyes in a bit of disgust. She could detect the foul scent of sleep and liquor as soon as he cracked his mouth open to reply.

"Rocko is on the phone. It's important."

She handed him the phone and he slowly took it.

"What's up?" he asked groggily into the phone.

"Cuz. Wake up. We had an incident."

"What kind of incident?" Niko asked, slowly coming to.

"The babysitter called out sick," Rocko replied.

They always spoke in code over the phone. Niko knew exactly what that meant. He didn't hear it often, but when he did, it made the hairs stand up on his body. He immediately sat straight up. He was now all ears.

"What's she sick with? Did she say?" Niko inquired.

He wanted to know who had pulled her over. Was it the state police, city police, or worse ... the Feds? There were so many different scenarios that it could be. He needed answers right away.

"I'll be there in thirty-minutes. We'll discuss everything then, Rocko said before disconnecting the call.

ROCKO GOT TO NIKO'S HOUSE IN LESS THAN TWENTY MINUTES. Even though he was there on serious business, he couldn't help but admire the sprawling estate as he pulled up. He always did. Niko lived in the suburbs of Birmingham in a 5,000 square feet Mediterranean style home. Even at the dead of night, the estate was remarkably beautiful. Original Moravian and Indian tiles, a limestone fireplace and skylight, marble countertops, beautiful arches connecting the dining and family room --- The home was top of the line. Tucked in a gated community, and surrounded by lush landscaping, the home was nothing short of exquisite.

Rocko noticed the lights on in the front part of the home when he got out of his car. He wasn't surprised that Niko was already waiting in the living room for him. To his surprise, Carmen was also up as well.

"What's up, Niko?" Rocko greeted his cousin somberly after walking inside.

"Hey, Carmen. I'm sorry to disturb y'all at this time of night, but it's kind of urgent," he said, as he made his way into the house.

Rocko gave Niko a look. Niko knew what the look meant. He didn't need to say anything else. Niko knew that whatever Rocko had to say, he didn't want to say it in front of Carmen. It wasn't that he didn't trust Carmen; he just didn't want her asking a bunch of questions, nor did he want her possibly running back and repeating anything that was said.

When it came to Carmen, there was always a conflict of interest. Although Niko was her husband, her brother Diego was their plug, supplying him with more work than they knew what to do with. Before meeting Carmen five years ago, Niko sold weight in the Birmingham area. He always had dreams of expanding. A chance meeting with the beautiful Carmen would prove to change his life in ways he never dreamed.

5'2 with thick, beautiful brown hair, Carmen seemed out of place at the predominately black night-club that she'd accompanied her college friend to. Looking like a cross between Vanessa Bryant and Jennifer Lopez, every man up in the place was mesmerized by her beauty. While she had their attention, there was only one man, that grabbed hers.

Although Niko had met his fair share of beautiful women, it wasn't often that he ran into the sister of a Mexican drug dealer.

Initially drawn in by her exotic beauty, Niko quickly knew something was different about Carmen. Unlike most college girls, she never once complained about her tuition, room, and board. She also drove around care-free in a $100k BMW i8. Curiosity kept Niko around until he was in good enough to meet her family. As soon as he realized he was dating the sister of a Spanish drug boss, it was nothing but up from there.

Niko would treat Carmen like a princess if he had to get what he wanted. He showered her with love, affection, and gifts before finally making her his wife. The whole time, her brother Diego was flooding him with more drugs than he could handle. Once he brought in Rocko to help him become more organized and expand into Atlanta, he would see his organization catapult to the top. Carmen and Rocko were his superpowers.

Unfortunately, unhealthy habits and poor choices had them in situations like the one they were in tonight. Like any other issue they faced in the drug game, Carmen couldn't be too informed on what was going on. There was no way that they wanted her thinking that they didn't have things under control. If for any reason she felt that way, she would surely advise her brother. They didn't want him thinking that his organization could also be in jeopardy along with theirs.

"Babe can you give us a minute?" Niko asked her.

"Yeah. I'm gonna go back upstairs and lay down anyway. Come up when Rocko leaves," she said as she stood on her tiptoes to lean in and give her husband a kiss on the cheek.

As soon as Carmen was gone and they heard the bedroom door close, Niko began rambling off a barrage of questions.

"What the fuck is going on?" he asked his cousin.

The look on his face told him that it wasn't good news. He knew it couldn't possibly be good news anyway since Rocko and woke him out of his sleep and drove to his house at the ass crack of dawn.

"Luscious crashed the whip, and they found all the drugs in the car. The Feds picked her up."

"Fuck!" Niko growled.

"Is she talking?" he asked, immediately preparing himself for the worst-case scenario.

"It's even worse than that," Rocko replied. "She's out."

"How the fuck did she get out after getting knocked with over twenty keys?"

"I don't fucking know. That's what I'm trying to get to the bottom of right now. Zoe talked to her, but she was so rattled that she didn't get any information that was valuable. She knows that Luscious agreed to work with them. What she's already told them, we're unclear of. Our main concern is that the bitch is out, and she's scared. We got a big problem Niko," he reiterated for emphasis.

He wanted to be extra sure that his cousin was getting the message through his thick, hard head.

"She's not like those other bitches that you can manipulate into taking a charge for you. I have a strong gut feeling that sis is going to fold under pressure. And on top of that, Zoe is saying she's pregnant. Why the fuck didn't you tell me that?"

"Nigga, I ain't gotta tell you I got another stripper bitch pregnant," he whispered, getting closer to Niko to speak. "And lower your fuckin' voice. Carmen isn't that far. It'd be just my luck that she was somewhere listening."

His eyes quickly scanned the room. Even though the door was closed, he waited a few seconds before he began speaking again.

"I thought I had it under control," he admitted.

"Well, clearly you fuckin' don't," Rocko replied in annoyance. "Her being pregnant makes things even more complicated. She's not gonna want to sit in jail pregnant. As soon as you found out, you should have taken her off the runs. Damnit Niko!"

Rocko went over to the sectional and took a seat on the edge. It was so many thoughts going through his brain, he didn't know what to do.

"So, you know what that means if she's out, right?"

He looked to his cousin and waited for a response.

"Yeah, I know exactly what that means. She either gave us up, or she *agreed* to give us up ... Fuckkkk!" he yelled.

Unless they figured out what was going on and fixed the situation quickly. They were super fucked. In more ways than one.

"How the fuck did she get into an accident anyway," Niko wanted to know.

Zoe said she was on the phone with *you* right before it happened ... Smoke and Toots were in the background. You don't remember?" Rocko asked sarcastically.

"Yeah, I remember. She called me a few hours before you met us at the club," he admitted. "We exchanged words over this pregnancy shit. She wants to keep the baby and I don't. We got to arguing and she heard the two bitches in the background. Wanted to go back and forth so I just hung up on her."

Rocko stared at him like he'd lost his mind. Niko looked away.

"Nigga don't make this shit seem like it's my fucking fault. Yeah, I argued with the bitch on the phone, but that's because I was trying to get her to get an abortion. She started going off and acting stupid. I wasn't trying to hear that shit, so I hung up. Next thing you know, she's calling back, to back, to back. I'm hitting ignore. It never dawned on me that the bitch was on a run. She never should've been calling me in the first fucking place.

"Nigga you should have known she was going on a fucking run."

"You know nigga ... You seem to stay telling me what I should and shouldn't do. What I should fuckin' know, yet I don't see yo' ass keeping track of things either like you used to. The bitch only went off because she heard two chicks she knew in the background. Smoke and Toots were only there because you took forever to show the fuck up. Remember we waited hours for you to come through so we can run down the game like we always do. So, don't give me that bullshit. "

Rocko sighed. He knew his cousin was going to get defensive. He'd be lying if he even said he cared. Being irrational wasn't going to get them anywhere. Like always, he felt like he had to take charge.

"Look, there's no point of crying over spilt milk. Just start taking the necessary steps. Lay low. Don't answer any calls from Luscious and change your phone number."

"Nigga, you act like I'm new to this. Remember I was the one that taught you," Niko reminded him.

"Just let me handle it. It's Zoe's friend so I have a better chance of keeping tabs on her and finding out what's being said. We gotta handle this a little bit different ---"

Niko grew instantly irritated. Luscious was no exception. If she acted like she wanted to talk, she was gonna get dealt with just like anybody else would. He didn't give a fuck if it was Zoe's best friend --- sister or whatever the hell they wanted to call themselves. But ... to appease his cousin, he simply nodded his head along in agreement.

"I'm going to get Zoe to see what she can find out. See what Luscious really told them.".

"Yeah, please do so ... and quickly.

Rocko ignored his cousin and proceeded to exit his home. It was just like Niko to make demands when he was the largest part of the problem.

As Rocko sat in his car in silence and headed home, he knew that his time was up with his cousin. First it was Ms. Hattie, now Luscious. Too many slip ups and they were bound to go down. Rocko didn't need any more signs than that. God was trying to tell him something. Niko didn't listen to anything anyone said, and it was going to be his downfall. Rocko was determined not to fall with him.

"WHAT'S GOING ON?" CARMEN DEMANDED TO KNOW WHEN Niko finally stumbled upstairs into the room thirty minutes after Rocko had left.

"Nothing," he assured her. "Go back to bed.

"Don't tell me nothing, Niko. Rocko never stops by this late. He never looks that serious. Tell me what's going on."

"It's nothing that concerns you Carmen. Chill out," he said doing his best to ignore and move around her, so he could undress and finally get in the bed. He was tired, but as usual, she wanted to be up, following him around the room. In his face, asking questions about his business.

His business was none of her concern. The only thing she needed to be worried about was prancing around in the big ass house she insisted on having and spending up all his damn money on clothes and shoes. As beautiful as she was, it was unfortunate that her presence often annoyed him. She loved to be included in everything except when it came time for her to contribute anything of substance. As smart as she was, it was a shame that she wasn't putting that expensive degree to use.

"Don't tell me it's nothing that concerns me," Carmen replied sharply, her face flickering with anger. "If it's pertaining to your business, then it concerns me. If something goes wrong with your business, then it affects my family and that concerns me. Now tell me, what's going on."

Niko drew in a deep breath. She was starting to make him angry. She said the same thing every time she wanted to be nosey. She didn't need to know everything. She couldn't seem to understand that. Niko knew that she was fiercely loyal to her family, especially her brother. He took care of their entire family. He knew that if it ever came to it, she would choose her family without hesitation.

"Look ... We had a little situation okay. Nothing I can't handle. I'm on top of it and I have everything under control," he assured her.

"What type of situation?"

"A situation damn!" Niko snapped, before looking over at his wife and tempering his attitude. "Look, one of our runners got knocked. But Rocko and I have everything under control," he lied. "There's nothing to be worried about. If there is, you will be one of the first to know."

Carmen could sense her husband was lying, but she decided not to cause a stink about it. So, she said nothing as she lay back down in her bed to go back to sleep. She was going to wait and watch. During her years with him, she learned that Niko didn't do well under pressure. If he really had it under control, then he would be his regular self. If he didn't ... well, he would show it. Carmen knew a lot more than Niko thought she did, and she preferred it that way.

## ❦ 15 ❦

"How you feeling?" Zoe was seated on the living room sofa. She glanced at the wall clock. It was after 3 p.m. Luscious had been sleep all morning and afternoon.

"I'm okay. Just got a little morning sickness." She plopped down on the sofa a few inches from where Zoe was seated.

Zoe got up and went to make her something to drink. While Luscious slept, she had gone out and purchased her a few things to eat when she woke up. She pulled out the bottle of ginger ale that she had purchased and poured her a small cup. Emerging from the kitchen, she walked back into the living room and handed it to her.

"Here. Drink that. I heard you run to the bathroom and throw up a few times this morning. Gotta make sure you're keeping some water and Gatorade by your bed, so you won't get dehydrated." She sat back down. "That baby kicking yo' ass huh?" she asked with a smile.

"Yeah girl." Luscious forced a smile to her face. Truthfully, she wasn't feeling up to it.

"They called me thirty times." Luscious' face looked pained with worry.

"I know. I saw. The phone was ringing off the hook while you were sleep. Try not to let it worry you girl." As much as she wanted to comfort her friend, that was all she could come up with.

"I don't know how to do that." Luscious brought the cup of ginger ale to her lips and sipped from it. She then stared up blankly at the ceiling.

"Zoe ... as my friend, what do you think I should do?"

"Sweetie I can't answer that for you. I can't make that choice for you. There's a lot of factors you have to consider. You're pregnant. Do you want to give birth to your baby in jail? Fed cases take time. At least a year. What if they don't give you a bond. Then you have to consider how it's going to affect the baby if you go on the run. Yeah, you get to give birth at home, but what happens to your baby when you decide you want to face the shit. How are you going to feel giving that baby up to someone while you go sit? You know, if I'm here, I got your back 100%, but ultimately, you have the make the best choice for *you*."

Luscious sighed in frustration. She knew she had to decide very soon, and all the things that Zoe had just said, didn't do her much good.

"How long you think I can run?"

"Probably a long time if you leave early. You don't want to give them enough time to track you at all. You'd need a new social security card. A new birth certificate --- Cash."

"I think that's what I'm gonna do," Luscious finally admitted. "I want to talk to Niko first and see what he thinks."

"Luscious ... do you think that's a good idea? Can you really trust Niko?"

"Can you really trust Rocko?" Luscious countered sarcastically.

"Look, I'm not trying to argue with you. All I'm saying is, that nigga is going to make sure his ass is covered. He doesn't have to know that you're getting the fuck outta dodge. The less people that know where you're headed, the better your chances."

"I guess you're right. I'm gonna need cash tho' Zoe. Do you think you can get some from Rocko? To hold me over for a few weeks. At least until I can sit down and truly figure out what I'm going to do until then. These motherfuckin' Feds are on me girl. I don't have much time. I gotta get out of here."

"I'll talk to him. I'm sure it won't be a problem. You know I got you, no matter what."

"Thanks girl."

Zoe leaned down and gave her friend an emotional hug. "We gon' get through this," she said, releasing her. "I'm going home. I'm gonna go and talk to Rocko and see what he can do. I promise I won't be gone long," Zoe promised.

"Okay girl. Just hurry back. You know these crackers only gave me twenty-four hours. I need to move quick."

"I promise, I won't be long."

"BABY, PLEASE. I NEED TO TALK TO YOU FACE-TO-FACE." Luscious pushed her weave out of her face nervously, while she gripped her phone tightly and waited for Niko to respond.

Despite Zoe telling her that she needed to lay low and have zero contact with Niko, Luscious still called him. Zoe hadn't even been gone for five minutes before she was punching in his numbers and waiting for the call to connect.

Luscious was an emotional wreck and despite what her best friend thought was safest, she just wanted to confide in Niko and let him know what was going on. *Shouldn't he know what was going on?* Luscious thought to herself. After all, he was the father of her unborn child. Zoe should understand that. She had Rocko to talk to. To protect her. To guide her. She just wanted Niko to do the same thing. She wanted him to tell her that it was going to be okay. Tell her what she needed to do. Tell her things that he likely never would.

Sure enough, the guidance and words of reassurance from

Niko that Luscious desperately wanted and needed would never come. Despite Luscious telling him it was urgent that she speak with him face-to-face, Niko didn't even bother to respond. He instead, hung up in her ear. Perched on the edge of her bed, Luscious threw her phone to her side and began balling her eyes out. *Why the fuck me?* she thought, with her hands buried in the center of her palms. It seemed as if she were on a losing spree. Lately, she'd had nothing but non-stop bad luck.

A few minutes later however, her phone began to ring. She reached down and swiftly grabbed it. The number was unavailable. She immediately knew that it was Niko calling from a burner phone. She quickly swiped to answer it.

"If you talked to the fuckin' Feds, why the fuck would you call my number," Niko growled into the phone through gritted teeth without saying hello.

Luscious didn't even ask him how he knew. A part of her had the suspicion that Zoe was going to break her promise and tell Rocko. It didn't take him long at all to run his mouth to Niko.

"Babe, I didn't know what else to do. They were all over me. Hurling question, after question at me. They were gonna lock me up right then and there, pregnant or not."

It took everything out of Niko not to curse her all the way out. What made him even angrier was the fact that she called Zoe first and not him. Why the fuck did Rocko know before he did? She had no idea how bad that made him look. It made him look like he didn't have his business under control. For Luscious to be out was more of an insult. Most of the females he had running for him that he was also screwing, wouldn't dare say a word that would incriminate him. The more he thought about it, the more he realized that he didn't have his business under control, nor his women.

He didn't give a damn how pregnant Luscious was. She knew the rules. If she ever got caught during a run, she wasn't supposed to say a word. Lately, she was acting dumb as hell, forgetting everything she was taught. Calling his direct line after an encounter with the Feds. Luscious wasn't *becoming* a liability, she *was* a liability.

"What exactly did you tell them? And hurry up." He glanced at his real phone. Before he'd called her, he'd set his timer to sixty-seconds. He knew that burner phones were supposed to be untraceable, but he still wasn't taking any chances.

"They asked me for a name," she admitted. She figured she would lay it all out and tell Niko the whole truth. She hadn't even told Zoe this part yet.

"They asked me for the name of the person the drugs were coming from. They asked me where the drugs were headed to, and where they were coming from. They wanted to know the name of the person they were going to."

"What did you tell them? What name did you give them?" he demanded to know through clenched teeth.

Niko knew there were only two names that she could give them. She only knew the drugs were coming from Birmingham and going to Atlanta. She didn't know about stash-houses or meeting locations. She wasn't privy to all the other information."

"I--- I gave them your --- your name," she stammered.

"Fuck!" Niko was so angry he was shaking. He wanted to snap her neck, but he couldn't reach her through the phone.

"I only told them your nickname."

Niko scoffed. He paced the room he was in with his hands balled into fists. He didn't have a nickname. She was so stupid. Everybody called him Niko because that *was* his name. She was so busy fucking, sucking, and worrying about a dollar, she didn't even take the time to figure that out.

"Look ... you're home right?"

"Yeah."

"Stay where you are. We gotta get you the fuck out of there."

Niko glanced at his phone. The timer said he still had fifteen seconds.

"Luscious! Before you hang up. How much time did they give you?"

Niko knew all about how the Feds operated. When you agreed to work with them, they gave you a certain amount of time before they came to collect all the information that was promised to them.

"Twenty-four hours."

He sighed. "Okay, I'm on my way. I'm gonna take you to a safe house. It's a little way out, but nobody will be able to find you there." He paused for a second but then continued. "And Luscious. Don't tell anyone where you're headed. Not even Zoe okay."

Luscious agreed and then the call dropped. She rubbed her belly nervously. She hoped she was making the right decision.

৩৯৩

CARMEN HAD JUST STEPPED OUT OF THE SHOWER AND WAS headed into the bedroom when she heard Niko shuffling around inside their massive walk-in closet. Even though they were the only two people in the home, hearing her walk in startled him.

"Shit," he mumbled as the box he was digging through, dropped to the floor.

"What are you doing baby?" Carmen asked softly, walking up on him. She looked down on the floor and saw that Niko's small safe had fallen. Nearby also lay a silver handgun.

"Is that loaded?" Although she hated guns, she knew they were necessary for protection.

"No, it's not loaded." He reached down and scooped it off the floor. He stuffed it along the side of his belt buckle and pulled his Louis Vuitton t-shirt down over top of it.

"Is everything okay?" She knew it wasn't, but she asked anyway. It wasn't the first time that he had to handle a situation after a run gone bad.

"Yeah. I got everything under control," he assured her before kissing her forehead.

He went to walk off, but Carmen stopped him by wrapping her arms around his waist.

"You be careful okay. I know something's up. I gotta feeling." She stared into his eyes. She could see it.

"I told you not to worry. You let me do all the worrying." He looked away to break their gaze. He hated when she did that. It was like she could read him. See right through him. It wasn't much that he could hide from her.

"Okay baby. I won't worry. Just hurry home okay."

"I'll try," he lied. He knew he was going to be out for most of the night. He had some important business to tend to.

He hated what he had to do, but he knew it needed to be done. There was a snake in his camp, and there was only one way to get rid of it ... And that was to kill it.

## ❧ 16 ❧

"Have they reached out to her yet?" Rocko grilled Zoe as soon as she stepped foot in the house. He was sitting on the couch. The television was off, and the living room was quiet. It seemed as if he was waiting for her to walk through the door. She'd barely even had time to kick off her shoes before he came with all the questions.

"Yeah, they've been blowing her phone up all day."

"What did she tell them?"

"Nothing. She slept until after three. She didn't answer the phone. But like I told her, that's only going to hold them off but for so long. Eventually, they're gonna come looking for her. Probably pick her up. Force her to honor whatever she agreed to." Zoe plopped down on the loveseat across from the sofa that Rocko was sitting at. She curled her body up into the corner comfortably and looked over at Rocko.

"Damn ... So, what's she gonna do?" he pried. He had no doubt that Zoe knew more than what she was telling, and he planned to get it out of her.

"Honestly ... I think she's going to run."

"What!"

"What other choice does she have babe? She's pregnant, stressed, and terrified."

"Why doesn't she just keep quiet and let us handle the legal shit. Niko knows some of the best lawyers in the state of Alabama ... Shit, he knows some of the best lawyers in the country. If she faces the shit, I have no doubt that she's going to get off."

"That's the problem Rocko. It's easy for you to act like you're so sure that she's going to get out, but you're really not. I get it ... Nobody wants her to say anything that's going to incriminate anyone else. But shit ... she doesn't want to sit in a fuckin' jail cell behind your sorry ass cousin."

"Wait ... *My sorry ass cousin.* What does that mean? Your homegirl knew the risks when she signed up and began accepting *my sorry-ass cousin's* money. It wasn't his fault that she got into an accident and they found an ass load of drugs. It was hers. Now she doesn't want to man up and face the shit like an adult. How is that playing fair."

Zoe sighed. Everything her man was saying was right. Noticing her becoming emotional, Rocko softened up.

"Look, I know this is hard, baby, but no one that chooses to participate in this game can pick and choose when they want to be solid. Nor can they pick and choose the circumstances that they want to be solid under. Yeah, my cousin is a dog ass nigga, but Luscious knew that when she started fuckin' with him. A lot of females hop in this shit because of the fast cash. They think that just because they throw a little pussy at Niko, he gon' be pussy whipped and gon' make choices that are in his and her best interests. That's where they fuck up. They get so caught up and forget what their role really is. I done seen that shit happen far too many times."

Rocko wasn't lying when he said that. Niko had fucked countless runners, with several of them getting jammed up and caught on runs with his drugs. It never failed that every single time, they were expecting special treatment because they were sleeping with him. Unfortunately, they never got it. Rocko was surprised none of the situations had backfired sooner. He knew that it would only take one bitter, heart-broken woman to come in and turn their organization upside down.

"My cousin is always gon' put his business and family over any broad that runs for him. Even if he's sleeping with her. Now you see why I didn't want you doing it," he reminded her. "You sign up as a crash-dummy from the get-go."

Rocko knew that his cousin was a catastrophe waiting to happen.

"But we gotta help her Rocko. She's my best friend. My sister," Zoe said with tears welling up in her honey-brown eyes.

Rocko sighed. "What do you need me to do?"

"Well ... She only has two choices. She can either run *or* face it. Given her mental state, I don't think the latter is going to be a good choice right now."

"Why do you say that?" Rocko's brows furrowed curiously.

"Because she's angry at Niko. She's not going to be loyal to a man that's done nothing but give her his ass to kiss." She took a deep breath but then decided to be completely honest. "The only way Luscious was able to get out of there without handcuffs is because she gave them a name."

Rocko stood up abruptly from his spot on the couch. "And whose name was that?"

"Niko's. They wanted to know who the drugs came from and she told them Niko."

"Fuck," he grumbled in frustration. He wondered if that was the only name she'd told them. "Why would she tell them that babe?"

Rocko got up and began pacing the living room while Zoe sat in the corner of the loveseat nervously.

"It was her only choice."

Rocko wanted to curse and knock shit over. *It wasn't her only choice*, were his thoughts. She had other choices. She took the easiest route. He had to let his cousin know what was going on.

They also had to face the reality that she likely told them more. At this point, they couldn't trust Luscious. She knew too much. Rocko decided right then and there that he was done. If the Feds started rounding nigga's up, he was good as done.

"Babe, why don't you call Luscious? She's gonna need to skip town until we figure some things out. Let her know she doesn't need to worry about money, I'll take care of it."

Zoe jumped from the table and ran to grab her phone. That's exactly what she was waiting to hear. She was going to get around to asking him to help on the cash tip; however, he beat her to it. Now that Rocko was starting to panic, so was she. They had to help Luscious get away from Birmingham, or her man could possibly go down.

❧

"Nigga we got a huge problem," Rocko stated before Niko could even so much as utter a hello.

"Doesn't sound good. I'm gonna call you right back," Niko said to his cousin before hanging up.

A minute later, he called Rocko back on another burner phone. Luckily for him, he had plenty of them at his disposal.

"I'm assuming you talked to your girl?" Niko said as soon as the call connected.

"Yeah. It's worse than we thought. She gave them your name."

Silence fell over the line.

"Did you hear me?" Rocko asked.

"Yeah, I heard you. Shit is bad. What else is your girl saying?"

"That she's not trying to sit in jail pregnant and that she wants to run. I'm pulling out some cash from my safe now. I'm gonna have Zoe go pick her up, and they're gonna meet me so I can get her to a safe house somewhere far. Get her some new paperwork and social security cards. She needs to disappear off the face of the Earth."

"Facts, I agree." Unfortunately, Niko agreed in an entirely different way.

"Look, we'll be fine if we control the situation. If she runs, we take her or send her off to where she's running. If we can control her movement and control her cash flow, we'll be fine. If we can't, and the Feds get to her before we do, we're fucked."

"Right, but we gotta do it quick. She only has twenty-four hours. The Feds are going to be banging on her door real soon."

"Yeah, you're right. I have Zoe calling her now. She'll probably go pick her up in about an hour or two. Give her some time to get herself together and grab what she needs to grab."

"Alright cuz. Keep me posted. And Rocko ... I appreciate you handling things for me. I owe you," Niko said.

"Don't worry about it man. But we do gotta sit down and discuss some changes that need to be made."

"Bet," Niko agreed before they both hung up.

Niko dropped the burner phone down into the passenger seat and looked at the time. Because he lived deep in the suburbs, it was going to take him another thirty minutes to get to Luscious. All he had to do was scoop her up and head out. He'd called her back and told her he was on his way and to be ready. They just had to be long gone by the time Zoe returned.

⚜

LUSCIOUS BIT THE CORNERS OF HER FINGERNAILS AND nervously paced the floor of her living room. She was waiting on Niko to arrive and get her far away from Birmingham. She looked down at her phone. It was on the coffee table vibrating and going off non-stop like crazy. She'd gotten dozens and dozens of calls from the Feds. Zoe had also been blowing her up for the past fifteen-twenty minutes. She picked up the phone when she realized a text had come in.

*Rocko's going to give you as much money as you need. I'm coming to get you and he's gonna get you set up somewhere safe. I'll be there in an hour.*

Luscious sat the phone back down on the coffee table and went back to pacing. Then something hit her. She suddenly stopped. Things didn't make sense. Rocko and Niko usually ran everything past one another. It was odd that they didn't seem to be doing that now. Rocko was sending Zoe to get her, while Niko was in route to get her too. Something was up. Luscious' lips began to tremble, while her heart began to pound as she realized for the very first time, she didn't know who to trust. She loved Zoe, but she didn't trust Rocko. Even though she had told Zoe not to tell anyone what she'd told her, she still did. That right there was causing her to question her loyalty.

Who was Zoe more loyal to? Her or Rocko? She hated to acknowledge the fact that it was now probably going to be Rocko. With a few sweet words, he'd probably convinced Zoe to tell him everything. In a situation like the one they were in now, there was no telling what either of the men would do to protect themselves and their freedom. Rocko knew that her and Zoe were extremely close, so if he wanted to do something to her, then he would likely use Zoe to do it. Of course, Zoe wouldn't have the slightest clue.

Niko too, was also acting weird. He'd called and told her to make sure she was ready. He also reiterated the request that she not tell anyone that she was meeting up with him or that he was coming to get her. Everything just seemed way too odd. It seemed like both Niko and his cousin were way too eager to get her in their possession. For the first time in a long time, Luscious felt like she was in grave danger.

## 17

"Luscious!" Zoe called out after returning back from her own home. She'd just walked into the house, and after doing a brief walk-through, she didn't see or hear her anywhere. "Luscious!" she called out again. Still no answer.

It was weird. She'd called her friend numerous times before she'd left and for whatever reason, she wasn't picking up. She'd even texted her, but that too went unanswered. She had only been gone a little over an hour. She wasn't sure where Luscious could have got to that quickly.

Zoe walked into Luscious' room, the bathroom, and even her own former bedroom. Her friend was still nowhere in sight. She walked over to the window and peered out the blinds into the parking lot. Luscious car was still parked in the same spot it was in earlier.

"What the fuck is going on?" she asked aloud.

She dug in her purse and pulled out her cell phone again. She dialed Luscious phone number once more and waited for it to ring. This time however, it went straight to voicemail. *What the fuck?* Zoe thought. She tried dialing the number another two times. Same thing. Zoe sighed and walked into the kitchen. She needed something to drink to help wash down the feeling of dread that now sat in the pit of her stomach. She didn't know what was going on and she was starting to worry.

After opening the cabinet and pulling out a glass, she opened the fridge and filled it up with cold water from a pitcher that sat inside. As she took small sips from the glass, she saw something that she hadn't noticed earlier. Luscious' purse. *Where would she go without her purse?* she wondered.

Zoe sat down her glass so she could go and retrieve the purse from where it was sitting in the corner of the kitchen counter. She opened it up, dug through it, and realized Luscious' keys were still in there. Her wallet was also still inside. She quickly snatched it out and opened it up. All her credit cards were neatly tucked into the folds.

"Shit," she mumbled in frustration. Something was going on. Something was wrong. There was no way that Luscious would leave without taking the things most important to her travels. Things she'd need to get by. How was she getting around with no car or car keys? She didn't have any money. No credit cards. It didn't make any sense. Things weren't adding up. Luscious had specifically stated that she needed money to get away earlier that day. Rocko was currently rounding up enough cash to hold her over for a month. How could she just leave without it?

Zoe paused for a minute and then it suddenly hit her that Luscious had probably done one of two things. She'd probably called Niko and left with him, *or* she'd left with the Feds. Just as the thought of the Feds entered her mind, she got the idea to thoroughly search Luscious' wallet. She scrounged around in it for a minute and finally found what she was looking for. It was a business card located in the zippered section of her wallet. *Agent Sterling.* That was the name on the card. She stuffed it into her pocket. Realizing that she wasn't going to accomplish anything still standing there, she left and headed home. She had a lot of questions for Rocko.

ZOE WALKED INTO THE HOUSE SHE SHARED WITH ROCKO AND
noticed it was unusually quiet. As she walked further inside, she
could hear the water running. She walked through the house and
headed to the bathroom that the sound was coming from.
Noticing that the door was slightly ajar, she peeked inside and
saw Rocko taking a shower. He didn't see her. Normally the sight
of his naked silhouette would entice her to step out of her own
clothes to join him; however, today was different. Her mind was
in a whole other place.

She parted her lips, about to call out to him. But instead
decided that she wouldn't disturb him. She would let him take
his shower in peace and then talk to him when he got out.

Zoe walked down the hall and into their massive bedroom
and noticed Rocko's phone sitting on the nightstand where he
always left it. For a minute, she just stood and stared at it. She
never went through his phone. She hated going through his
things. Up until today, he'd never given her a reason to want or
need to.

Zoe picked up the phone, unlocked it, and then began to
scroll through it. She knew Rocko wasn't stupid enough to send
any incriminating text messages to his cousin. She didn't care,
because that's not what she was looking for anyway. She just
wanted to see one thing. Something else. She continued scrolling
until she got to Rocko's call log. She studied it carefully. Just like
she suspected, he'd called Niko after she came in at the wee
hours of the morning. And he'd also called Niko right around the
time that she'd come back from Luscious' house the last time.
She knew it wasn't irony that he called him at those specific
times. Shit wasn't adding up and she planned to get to the
bottom of it.

She placed his phone back down on the nightstand and sat
quietly on the edge of the bed. She was going to wait for him to

come out. Her friend had gone missing in action and she needed to know if Rocko or his cousin had anything to do with it.

Fifteen minutes later Rocko finally emerged from the bathroom with a towel wrapped around his body. He hadn't even completely dried off. Every step he took into the room, he left a droplet of water behind him.

"Hey baby." He smiled at the sight of Zoe. "I was just getting myself together before we head out." He didn't know the destination in mind for Luscious, but he figured they would probably drive her out somewhere far so she could lay low for a few days. At least until they were able to get her a new identification card and birth certificate so she could fly.

"We're not going to be heading out," Zoe replied, her face grim.

"What's the matter. Luscious change her mind?" he asked, still standing in the middle of the room.

"She's gone. I can't find her?"

"What do you mean, you can't find her?" Rocko asked, freezing in place.

"I went to her place. She wasn't there. Searched the apartment. Called her phone. It was ringing and then it started going straight to voicemail. Her car was still parked in the parking lot." Zoe drew in a deep breath and shook her head from side-to-side in frustration. All the stress was weighing heavily on her and had her beginning to feel ill.

"How does she just disappear without taking her car?"

"She didn't take anything. Her purse was still on the countertop. Her keys, credit cards. The little bit of cash that she had. Everything was still in there. I — I don't know," she stammered, growing more and more frustrated.

"What do you mean? Where could she have gone without taking any of her belongings?" Rocko asked, growing slightly impatient.

"I don't fuckin' know Rocko!" Zoe screamed. Her sudden

outburst was unexpected to both herself and him. He rarely saw Zoe upset.

"Zoe, you need to calm down and stop yelling. I'm just trying to figure things out. One minute you're telling me that she got busted by the feds, the next minute you're saying that she needs help getting somewhere safe, and now you're telling me that she's gone missing in action."

"That's exactly what I'm telling you Rocko. And since we're clarifying things, tell me how I asked you not to tell Niko anything, but you still took it upon yourself to call him as soon as I fuckin' left," she argued, her eyes darting over to his phone.

Rocko had been caught off guard and was now at a loss for words. He would have asked her how she knew but he already knew that she'd gone through his phone while he was away.

"You don't have anything to say about that tho' right?"

"Zoe, I'm sorry I broke your trust ---"

"I don't want to hear it Rocko. Now my friend has disappeared off the face of the fuckin' Earth and I have no idea where she could be. I trusted you." She looked at him with pain in her eyes.

"I know you did babe, but I had to let Niko know. This is bigger than just a broken promise. This is our lives. His life and my life are at stake. Luscious done already dropped the ball. We just trying to fix this shit."

"Fix it how? Where is my friend?" she cried out. Tears welled up in her eyes as she rose from her position on the bed and stared Rocko down. All kind of horrible thoughts scurried through her head.

"You think ...?" Rocko stood there for a moment and looked at Zoe. "You think I did something to Luscious?" he asked in disbelief.

"At this point, I don't know what to think anymore. I think it sounds really suspicious that I confide in you, you offer to help, and then suddenly my friend is nowhere to be found."

"Zoe, I swear I didn't have anything to do with your friend

being M.I.A. If something did happen, which it probably didn't, trust me when I say that we didn't have shit to do with it."

"You can only speak for yourself." Zoe stood and stared Rocko down icily.

"What's that supposed to mean."

"Exactly what I said. You can only speak for yourself. You definitely can't speak for your cousin."

"Zoe ... Me nor my cousin did anything to Luscious okay. I mean, come on, she was pregnant with Niko's baby."

"A baby that he didn't want. Look, Niko ... Just help me find her okay," Zoe stated firmly. She was done going back and forth with Rocko. She spun around on her heels and headed into the walk-in closet to grab the items she needed to take a shower. The day had been especially long and all she wanted to do was shower and relax.

While Rocko still stood in the middle of the room wrapped in a towel, she turned around to face him before heading out the room and into the bathroom.

"Talk to your cousin for me. Find out if he's heard anything from Luscious."

She turned back around and walked out of the room. She was frustrated and worried, but she was going to take his word for now. That was all she could do. The first opportunity that she got; she was going to do some digging. There weren't too many places she could go or too many people that she could call. Luscious didn't have a relationship with her mother so she knew that she probably hadn't heard from her. There couldn't be too many places that she could be. Wherever she was, she was going to find her. She just had to start weeding them out one by one. She was going to start with Niko, and then she was going to put that card to use and find out what the hell they could tell her.

WITH A HEAVY HEART, ZOE LOOKED DOWN AT THE FIRST Response pregnancy stick for what seemed like the hundredth time. She usually didn't carry her purse into the bathroom but today she did. She was surprised that Rocko didn't notice. She'd only done it so she could hide her pregnancy tests at the bottom. She didn't want a whole lot of questions from him. Now certainly wasn't the time to have *that* discussion.

Zoe looked back down at the stick and sighed before placing it in the trash with the others. It was the fourth one she'd peed on. She wanted to make sure that it was accurate and that she was truly pregnant. Under any other circumstances, she would have been happy; however, she had far too much going on to be joyous about anything.

She picked up her phone from the bathroom counter and like she'd done for the twentieth time that day, she called Luscious. The line was no longer ringing; it was going straight to voicemail.

"Where are you girl? Please be okay," she said softly while staring at the beige wall.

She sat her phone back down and didn't even bother to leave a voicemail. She'd already left multiple. Something told her that Luscious was never going to respond. Something told her that something was wrong.

Zoe got up from where she was seated on the toilet and decided to head back into the bedroom and lay it down early. It was only a little after 7 p.m. but she'd had enough of the day anyway. There would be no lounging, cuddling, tv, or dinner. She had been nauseous most of the day and wasn't interested in much of anything, especially not food. Her nausea was what actually led her to grabbing the pregnancy tests after leaving Luscious' house. With everything that had been going on in her life, she hadn't even noticed that her cycle was past due. Seeing the positive tests staring at her from the trash can did nothing to ease her anxiety. She grabbed some tissue from the handle beside her, snatched some off, and threw it in the trash to cover them up. She didn't need the four reminders. She also didn't need Rocko seeing them. She needed to digest things and then she would decide on when and how to tell Rocko.

She wasn't nervous about telling him anything. She knew Rocko would be a good dad. Her main issue was she was no longer sure about who Rocko was outside of being her man. While she hated to think he had anything to do with Luscious going missing or knowing anything about her going missing, she had to consider it. Who was Rocko? *Really.* Was he really the loving Birmingham thug that captured her heart, or was he a ruthless thug that would do whatever it took to cover up the dirt he did? Was like his cousin? Zoe was unsure about all these things. And for her to have a baby around him, she needed to be.

Zoe grabbed her things and returned to her room where she found Rocko lying in bed half sleep.

"That was a long shower," he said sleepily from the bed.

"Yeah. Was just doing some thinking," she admitted.

She walked into their closet and put away her things. When she came out, she stopped at the mirror and began brushing her hair around her head to form a wrap.

"I'm a little tired myself. It's been a long day."

"Yeah. Me too. I been feeling tired myself."

After Zoe tied her hair up in a silk scarf, she climbed into the bed. Rocko wasted no time sliding under her and throwing his arm around her waist. He kissed the back of her head softly.

"I don't like to argue with you, Zoe. I love you, and I hope you know that. I would never do anything to hurt you and I would never do anything to someone you love because I know that would hurt you. I don't know where Luscious is, but I'm gonna ask questions and do whatever I need to do to help you find her," he promised.

Zoe didn't respond right away. Everything in her wanted to believe him. Her eyes glistened as emotions overcame her.

"You hear me, Zoe?" Rocko asked, his voice groggy from sleepiness.

"Yeah, I hear you babe."

"I love you."

"I love you too, Rocko." Zoe meant every word. She just hoped he meant every word of what he'd just said as well.

৩৯৩

AFTER TOSSING AND TURNING IN THE BED FOR HOURS, ZOE tiptoed out of her home and was now sitting in her car contemplating whether she should do what she was about to do. Her friend was weighing heavily on her mind. It was almost impossible for her to sleep not knowing if she was okay. Zoe needed to know something --- anything. There was no one to call to even check and see if they'd heard from Luscious. She didn't have a good relationship with her mother, so there was no point in calling her. That would probably be the last person she called if she were in trouble. She wasn't close to any of her siblings, so Zoe figured it would be useless to call them as well.

Zoe looked down at her phone and checked the number to make sure it was correct before she dialed it. Sure enough, it was correct. Zoe pressed the little green circle with the phone symbol in it to dial the call. After a few rings, a crisp, Caucasian sounding voice picked up.

"Agent Sterling."

Zoe hesitated after hearing an actual person pick up the line. For a moment she started to chicken out and hang up the phone. But if she did that, she knew that she would be still stuck in the same boat, with no idea on the whereabouts of her friend. She needed answers and she needed them now. She knew that the longer a person goes missing, the less likely you were to find them.

"Umm, hi. My name is Zoe. My friend is um ... missing and I found your card in her purse. Her name is Luscious. I'm sorry. That's her stripper name. Her real name is Monica Baily. I know

135

there's probably not a lot you can tell me, but I need to know if you know where she is? Have you seen or spoken to her?"

Zoe paused. If she was speaking to the right person, she didn't want to say too much. She couldn't let the agent know that she knew what was *really* going on. She didn't want her to know that she knew the real reason why the card was in her purse."

"Monica Bailey? I actually do know her and have spoken to her in the past few days. I'm sure Ms. Bailey has filled you in on why she would be in contact with us."

Zoe went to speak but Agent Sterling cut her off.

"You don't have to say anything. As a matter of fact, I know you probably won't."

Agent sterling paused for a moment. She wanted to be sure that her words left a lasting impact on the young girl. She could tell that she was worried sick, and she also couldn't help but detect the sound of fear in Zoe's young voice.

"Ms. Bailey is not with us. Quite frankly, we've been looking for her and lost contact with her yesterday afternoon. If you see her or hear from her, please talk to her. She's in danger and we are her best chance at safety."

"What do you mean? Why would she be in danger?"

"Because the people that she can harm with the information that she knows, are dangerous. Her, her family, people closest to her, are all going to be in danger until we get them off the streets. If you know anything ... anything at all. Please tell us. Because as Monica's friend, you're potentially in just as much danger as she is."

Zoe swallowed the hard lump in her throat. She felt sick to her stomach. For all she knew, the bitch could be lying. That's what the Feds did ... they lied. Right?

"I just want to ask you again, Zoe. Do you know anything at all?" Agent Sterling asked. The hesitation from Zoe is exactly what she wanted. That's exactly what she was looking for.

"N-No," Zoe stammered. "Not yet anyway."

"Well please remember my name and number. If you think of anything or learn anything new, please don't hesitate to give me a call."

"And you do the same, please. If Luscious, I mean Monica, shows up or contacts you, please call me. I just want to make sure she's okay."

"I will, Zoe. And one last piece of advice. If you are around the same people that Monica was dealing with, be careful."

"Believe me, I will," Zoe promised.

"Before you go, Zoe ... since I have you on the phone, do you mind if I ask you a few questions?" she started.

Before Zoe had the chance to decline, Agent Sterling started right back up.

"Luscious is your best friend, and I know you're worried about her. We are too. We're worried about what may have happened to her. Are you familiar with, or do you know her boyfriend Niko King?"

"Unfortunately, not really," she admitted as she clutched the phone in her hand. She really didn't know much about Niko other than the fact that she couldn't stand him.

"Well what about his business partner and cousin, Rocko King?"

"Agent Sterling ... if you don't mind. I gotta go. I'm sorry I can't be of much help to you."

"I'm sure you can. You just don't want to be," Agent Sterling replied sharply.

Zoe paused for a second and realized she'd made a mistake. The Feds always knew more than what they pretended to know. They always had one up on you.

"I know that Monica was dating Niko and that you are dating his business partner Rocko. Monica didn't have to tell us that for us to know. Did Luscious, or Monica tell you that they've both had federal drug cases against them before? Did she tell you that Niko was married? Did she also tell you that Rocko was married?" she asked.

Zoe's heart sank to the bottom of her stomach. It felt like she had been sucker-punched. Rocko was married?

"Umm, no. She didn't tell me any of those things and frankly, it's none of my business. I'm sorry to have disturbed you, Ms. Sterling," Zoe said quickly. She'd gotten a lot more than what she bargained for by calling. All she wanted to know was if her friend was okay. She just wanted to feel better, so she could sleep. Instead, she felt worse.

"You're not disturbing me. When you're ready to have a full conversation, don't hesitate to call. And one final word of advice. Make sure you truly know the men you hang around. Make sure you look out for yourself."

"Thank you for taking my call. You have a good night Agent Sterling," Zoe said before hanging up.

For a few minutes, Zoe sat in the parking lot quietly peering out the window. There wasn't much to look at other than a lot full of fancy cars. She looked up at the big expensive building that Rocko had her living in. Her bed was in there and so was her man, but she had no desire to go back inside. *Rocko is married.* Out of all the things that bitch had just said on the phone, that stuck out to her most. She was sure he had an explanation. Why wouldn't he tell her he was married. It didn't make sense. What was he trying to cover up? Was he still with her? Did he still take care of her? Zoe had so many questions. Her heart ached. The man she loved had lied to her, and she didn't understand why. He constantly told her to open up. Yet he himself failed to disclose such important information.

Zoe looked down at the passenger seat. She had her purse. That's all she needed. She didn't know who anyone was anymore. She wondered if Luscious had known. She wondered if she would have told her if she did. Did Luscious really have her best interest at heart? She didn't know who to trust anymore. She didn't even know if she was safe. If Luscious had disappeared while she was pregnant, what made her any different.

Zoe looked at the time on the dash. It was well after

midnight. She had class in the morning, but she wasn't going. She would email her professor in the morning and let her know she had an emergency. She had to get away. She had a baby growing in her stomach that she needed to protect. If leaving and starting over was what she had to do ... then so be it.

## ❧ 18 ❧

"Zoe," Rocko called out for the third time. He'd just woken up and Zoe wasn't beside him where she usually was. That was strange. He gazed out the window and noticed that the sun was breaking through the clouds. His eyes shifted over to his phone. He picked it up and checked the time. It was 6 a.m.

*Where the fuck could she be?* He slid from under the covers and got up to search the apartment. After walking around and checking every inch of the house twice, he still couldn't locate her. He decided he was just going to call her.

Rocko dialed her number and waited for it to connect; however, an automated voice popped up instead.

*The number you've dialed is no longer in service.*

He hung up. Panic and worry instantly fell over Rocko. *What the fuck is going on?* he thought. Even though her number was programmed in his phone, he still called her again. As he paced his bedroom floor, he thought to himself, *Maybe it was an error.* There was no way Zoe's phone could be off. He remembered that she had just paid her phone bill. She wouldn't just change her number. He would be the first to know. Unfortunately, it continued to say the same thing.

"The fuck!" Rocko yelled out unexpectedly, his broad chest

rising and falling heavily from a mixture of frustration and anticipation.

He threw his phone on the bed and walked into the closet. All of Zoe's belongings were still there. She hadn't taken anything. Even her favorite sandals that she wore almost daily were still there. He would often tease her about how she was wearing them out.

Coming out of the closet, Rocko went and sat on the bed. He was trying to get his thoughts in order, but it was difficult. He bit down on his bottom lip in worry while he tried to think of where Zoe could have gone. Why would she even leave? Wasn't she happy? Was there something that he didn't know.

He remembered she had taken a shower and then laid down. She seemed fine. She didn't give him any indication that she was upset. He did remember that their last argument about Luscious was a bit explosive. Could she have left me over that? he wondered. He remembered her asking him if he knew where Luscious could be. Did she suspect him? Did she fear him? Was she in fear of someone? All those questions swarmed his brain at once.

Rocko got up from the bed and headed to the bathroom. Worrying about Zoe had him forgetting to take his morning leak. When he walked in the bathroom, he noticed there was a small piece of trash in the floor. He went to pick it up and thought that was strange. He was very meticulous and although Zoe would often hurl around her things, she was fairly neat herself. She wouldn't just leave trash in the floor. After picking it up he noticed the trash was actually the corner of a box. He recognized the brand. It was one he was familiar with. He had purchased it before.

Rocko went over to the trashcan. He looked down and noticed a fistful of toilet paper was at the top. It was like someone just threw it on top to conceal something. Not thinking, he dug in the trash and pushed the toilet paper to the side. Just like he suspected, there was a box and several pregnancy tests at the bottom. He didn't even need to pick either of them up to see the two bright pink lines on all of them. *Zoe is pregnant.*

The newfound revelation caused a mixture of emotions for him. He would be happy if he knew where she was ... but he didn't. She was pregnant and had just up and disappeared. There had to be an explanation. It was all just so uncharacteristic of her. He was happy but he was worried, and unfortunately, the worry was outweighing everything.

Something was up, and he was going to get to the bottom of it.

ॐ

NOT EVEN THIRTY MINUTES HAD PASSED SINCE ROCKO discovered Zoe's positive pregnancy test in the bathroom. He was now fully dressed and racing down the highway to his cousin's house. Several times, Zoe had questioned the character of his cousin. For the first time, Rocko couldn't help but to do so as well. Niko had the most to lose. Both women going ghost at the same time just didn't sit well with him. The longer he drove and the closer to his cousin's house he got, the angrier Rocko became. He prayed that Niko hadn't done anything stupid or crazy.

Rocko knew that Niko had done things in the past. Things that had nothing to do with him, but everything to do with the business. People had come up missing. People had come up dead, and plenty of times, witnesses had recanted their statements. Rocko never asked questions. He just charged it to the game. That wasn't the side of the business that he participated in. He just knew that it was necessary. Rocko just prayed that the necessary hadn't occurred again.

Rocko pulled up to Niko's house a few minutes later. He spun into the driveway and hopped out of his car. He didn't even bother to cut it off. He let his door slam with the keys still dangling from the engine. After banging on the door like the police, he wasn't surprised when Niko came to the door with a scowl on his face and his gun in his hand.

"Nigga what the fuck is wrong with you, banging like you the damn cops?" he asked, letting Rocko in. He could tell that his cousin was upset about something. The serious look on his face told it all.

"Zoe is gone. I can't find her or reach her," Rocko huffed.

Niko closed the door and turned around to face his cousin. He put down his gun on the table by the door and studied Rocko's face.

"And?" he asked blankly.

"The fuck you mean *and?*" Rocko countered, becoming even angrier by Niko's blatant lack of concern.

"Nigga, you worried about the wrong shit. You come banging on my door like it's life and death and it's about a bitch."

Out of instinct, Rocko ran over to where Niko was standing and got right up in his face. His jaws were tight, and his fists were balled at his sides. He wanted to knock his cousin clean out.

"Nigga don't ever disrespect me or her like that again in your motherfuckin' life! Zoe ain't just some bitch. I love her nigga. She's carrying my fuckin' child and I want her back. Wherever the fuck she at. So, I'm either gon' find her ... Or they gon' find you," he said coldly, with a murderous glare in his eyes.

Niko stared in Rocko's eyes and knew that he was dead serious.

"Find me huh? So, you think I got something to do with her being gone?"

"I don't know what to think Niko ... One-minute shorty come up missing, and the next minute, my girl who also happens to be her best friend and patna, comes up missing too? Shit sound like it stink to me. Zoe didn't take no clothes. Nothing. Just her car and her purse."

Niko smirked and studied his cousin. "So, just because both

of them gone, that mean I got something to do with it. Nigga, either you a plum dumb fool or you real pussy whipped."

Rocko returned his stare and didn't budge. "If something happened to her, then I know you had something to do with it. I meant every word I said nigga."

"You both need to calm down. You two are family, and I can hear you all the way upstairs." Carmen had emerged from the back room and was now trying to talk some sense into both men.

"My apologies Carmen. We're just having a disagreement." Rocko slowly backed out of his cousin's face. The last thing he needed was for the both to be going at odds in front of Carmen.

"Babe, I need to talk to my cousin alone." Niko glared at her. He had told her multiple times about butting in on his private business matters.

"Okay, but we need to talk when you're done talking to Rocko."

When Carmen finally exited the room, Niko turned to face his cousin. He had to get something off his chest even though he knew that Rocko wouldn't want to hear it. He knew that his cousin would never agree with what was really taking place.

"Rocko have you ever thought that maybe Luscious and Zoe played us?"

"What?" Rocko scoffed. "What are you talking about?" his brows furrowed.

"I mean ... what if the two of them played us? What if Luscious really didn't get knocked. What if they just took our shit and dipped. Beat us at our own game. Jacked us. It's funny how that bitch Luscious just ups and disappears and then Zoe goes missing too. Don't take nothing."

Rocko paused for a minute and stared at his cousin angrily. For some reason, he had a feeling that Rocko was trying to get in his head. That he was trying to manipulate him into believing some random scenario that he'd taken his time to come up with."

"That doesn't make any sense. Zoe would never do anything like that."

"How do you know that Rock?" Niko countered in exasperation.

"Look ... I just know that she wouldn't do no shit like that," Rocko continued to argue. "She's pregnant okay. I saw the pregnancy sticks in the bathroom. She left them there before she disappeared."

"What does that mean? That don't mean shit!" he argued. "The bitch Luscious said the same thing before she started talking this Fed shit. She said the same shit before she just up and disappeared too."

"Niko ... Cousin or no cousin, I don't know what type of shit you on, or what type of games you're playing, but she did not just run off with some bricks. That's not her, man," he argued. "She barely even asked me for shit. She was in her senior year of college. She wanted to make something of herself. I know that for a fact. I paid her final semester's tuition. She would not just up and leave that for some bricks. That's not her character."

Niko didn't respond.

"Make all the claims you want. I'm going to keep looking for her. And you better hope that I find her. I just pray you didn't do something you're going to regret," he stated coldly before walking out of the room and out of the home.

With gritted teeth, Niko said nothing. He just stood in the middle of the room where Rocko had left him. As much as he loved his cousin, he prayed that his blind love for Zoe, didn't force his hand.

# ❧ 19 ❧

Rocko pulled slowly into the dirt parking lot and placed his car in park. He looked down at his phone to make sure he had the correct address. It was right. The numbers in his phone matched the numbers on the front door.

The cluster of apartments were a dingy white and had two levels. The rows of apartments resembled a motel and was almost set up like one. The only way Rocko could confirm they were apartments is because there was a sign out front that said so.

Rocko hopped out his truck, locked his door and headed to the second floor of the first building he saw.

"You got some change sir?" a random, homeless-looking black man hanging by the stairwell asked him. He was old and feeble, and his soiled clothes had seen better days.

Rocko dug in his pants and handed him some. He would have given him more, but he didn't want to wind up getting robbed. He was no sucka, but he had just pulled up in a Mercedes truck, smack dab in the hood. Birmingham and its surrounding area were rough. He didn't want to become a victim by being too generous.

Apartment 203 was the one he was searching for. As soon as

146

he came to it, he tapped a few times and waited. About a minute later, a woman's voice called out to him.

"Who is it?" Nora didn't wait for him to respond. Instead, she swung the door open and stood there and stared him down.

"Uh, how you doing? I'm uh—" he started, but Nora cut him off.

"I know who you are. Come in." she said dryly. She opened her door and gave Rocko enough room to walk inside.

"What brings you here?" she asked once he was fully in. She closed the door and walked into the front room with Rocko trailing closely behind her. She couldn't help but notice how fine he was. Zoe sure knew how to pick em.

"I hate to stop in on you without notice and involve you for matters like this, but your daughter just up and disappeared on me. Or, I guess you could say she went missing. I haven't seen her since last night."

Nora spun around to make sure she had heard him correctly. "You say she went missing?" Although she looked surprised, Niko noticed she didn't seem worried.

"Yeah. We went to sleep, and she was beside me, and when I woke up, she wasn't there. I tried calling her, but her phone is disconnected. I checked her closets and she didn't take anything with her. I don't understand."

Nora eyed the young man in front of her curiously. "You love her?" she asked, totally off topic.

Rocko stood at a loss for a second. He wasn't sure of the meaning behind her question. Of course, he loved her. He wouldn't be looking for her if he didn't. While Nora waited for his response she walked over to her folding table and retrieved her bottle of Tito's from it. She didn't even bother to get a glass. She twisted the cap off and threw some down her throat.

"Yeah, I love her," Rocko finally replied. He stared at Nora as she seemed to glide around the house. He wasn't impressed by her lack of hospitality, but she was interesting, nonetheless. Her mannerism and personality seemed completely different from that of her daughter's. Although their beauty was parallel.

"Unfortunate for you," she said. The response struck Rocko as odd. He began to question if stopping by Nora's had been a good decision. The lady seemed off.

"And why do you say that?"

"Because Zoe is ungrateful. The only person I ever see her show genuine love for, was my mother. God rest her soul."

"Ummm, I'm sorry Nora, right?" Rocko nodded. "I didn't come here to spark up feelings of resentment or anything. I just came to see if you had seen her. Maybe heard from her. I know you two don't have the best relationship or history, but I was hoping that you could help me find her. Or maybe, knew where she might be."

"I haven't seen Zoe since the day I found her fucking and sucking my man in my house."

"Excuse me?" Rocko coughed, completely caught off guard by Nora's statement.

"I haven't seen her since I caught her in my house sucking my man's dick. Believe me when I say honey, all that glitters isn't gold. You nigga's be thinking you got a prize just because a bitch pretty and young. Tuh," she scoffed. "Some prize huh? Now she done ran off on you and you come over here crying."

Rocko couldn't help but shake his head in disappointment. Bitter was an understatement. He didn't know how true Nora's statements were, but he certainly wasn't going to take her word over Zoe's. That would be a conversation for them to have on a later date. He couldn't help but feel sorry for Nora. As beautiful as she was, she was downright miserable. He could see it in her face and detect it in her words. He was sorry he ever came. Now he saw why Zoe came to him so vulnerable.

"I'm sorry you feel that way about your daughter. All I've known is the love she's shown me. Sorry for wasting your time," he said, before turning his back and heading back out the way he'd come.

"Try the country," Nora said unexpectedly, just as Rocko's hand was turning and pulling on the door handle.

My mother had a house in the country. Zoe grew up there. If she did run off and needed to clear her head, that might be a place she went."

"What's the address."

"205 Dakota Road."

"Thank you," Rocko replied before heading back to his truck.

Meeting Nora for the first time, made Rocko love her even more. He could only imagine how her life was growing up with that woman. He told himself that if he found her, he vowed to love her even harder.

# ❧ 20 ❧

Although the house was in poor condition and what some would even consider dilapidated, Zoe felt safe and at peace. The house itself was three bedrooms with one bathroom located on the top level. Right now, Zoe didn't mind the walk, but she knew the further along in her pregnancy she got, the more that was going to become a hassle. That's exactly why she was going to be contacting someone during the week to give her a quote to add a bathroom downstairs.

When her grandmother died, the one thing Nora did manage to do right was pay the property taxes on the old house that she owned. There was no way Nora was going to stay there but for whatever reason, she didn't want to lose it. Luckily for Zoe, her name was also on the deed, courtesy of her grandmother's will. As long as the property taxes were paid. Zoe would have a home. It was especially important to her since she had been briefly homeless. If only her mother had told her she had a home to go to after she kicked her out onto the streets. It wasn't until she did some digging that she found out that her name was on a piece of property.

Zoe planned to fix the place up and make it beautiful. She also planned to fill it with love. Something that it lacked when she was growing up. Zoe didn't have much money, but she did manage to save up from the allowance Rocko had been giving her. Once she graduated and started a new job, she would be fine. She planned to live here for as long as she needed.

She thought about school. She only had a month and a half left and was communicating with her professors so she could turn her work in online. She knew the material. She just needed to take the final exam. She had no doubt that she would pass each one with flying colors.

Zoe walked through the hall upstairs and headed through the bathroom. Since finding out she was pregnant she couldn't help but notice that her bladder was doing its own thing. Every time she turned around, she had to pee. As Zoe sat on the toilet, she thought she heard a vehicle's engine. That couldn't be. No one should be able to find her. No one knew about the house except her mother. The house was tucked in the rural parts of Birmingham. If you rode by it, you would miss it. The only way someone would notice it or find it, is if they were looking for it.

A few seconds later, Zoe realized that she wasn't hearing things when she heard a knock at the door. *Who the hell could that be?* she wondered, as she made her way downstairs to see.

෴

ZOE HAD ONLY BEEN GONE A DAY AND A HALF BUT ROCKO couldn't help but feel a sense of relief when the door swung open and she was standing there. When he first rode by it, he couldn't help but think the place was a borderline shack. He almost kept going. However, he'd stopped when he noticed the front of her car peeking out from where it was supposed to be hidden in the back.

"Zoe what the fuck babe?" Rocko rushed into the house and embraced her in a tight hug. "I was worried sick."

Zoe couldn't help but feel the stings of fresh tears creeping into the corners of her eyes. Rocko had been looking for her.

"Why did you leave." He paused and looked around. "Why are you staying here Zoe?"

"I --- I was scared. I didn't know what else to do. I'm pregnant and I just wanted to make sure that I was safe."

"Why wouldn't you be safe? I'm always going to make sure you're good. And I know you're pregnant. I saw the tests in the trash."

Zoe looked at Rocko and felt bad she doubted him. He had done nothing but show his love for her. However, she still had questions.

"The night I left, I couldn't sleep. Luscious was on my mind heavy. Earlier that day, I found a business card in her purse. It was for an Agent Sterling. I went outside to get some air and I decided to give her a call. I needed to know if Luscious was with them. I needed to know if she was safe. I didn't care if she was working with them, I just needed to know that she was safe."

"What did they tell you?" Rocko asked, now leaning up against the door while Zoe told her story.

"They said that she wasn't with them. She asked me if I knew Niko and she also asked me if I knew you."

Rocko's eyes widened. "She asked for me by name?"

"Yeah. She did," Zoe admitted. "I told her no and I tried to hurry her off the phone. But she tried to manipulate me to keep me on the phone. Keep me talking to her. She told me that I needed to be careful of you two."

Rocko shook his head angrily. He knew exactly what they were trying to do. They were trying to turn each person on the other. He wondered how much they really knew.

"She also told me that Niko was married ... and so were you."

Rocko swallowed the hard lump that had suddenly appeared in his throat. He knew that one day it was going to come out and he would have to explain to Zoe. He didn't know why he'd never told her. He should have a long time ago.

Rocko looked down and he could see the pain in her eyes.

She wondered what else he had lied about. What else he hadn't told her.

"Zoe ... I was married. I'm not anymore."

"Why wouldn't you tell me that? What's the big damn secret?" she demanded to know.

Just as Rocko was about to explain, his phone began to ring and vibrate in his pocket. He quickly dug down to retrieve it. He looked at the number.

"That's strange. It's Carmen, Niko's wife."

Zoe nodded for him to go ahead and take it.

Rocko quickly pressed accept and that's when his world seemed to stop.

"Rocko," Carmen sobbed into the phone. "I'm at the house! The police just busted through the doors! Please tell me Niko is with you. They're going to put me under arrest and lock me up!" she cried hysterically.

"Whoa, slow down, Carmen. The police are there? They're going to place you under arrest for what?"

"They claim they found drugs in the house. They have an informant Rocko. They said it's a woman that Niko was sleeping with."

All the color drained from Rocko's face. He hated that he had to do what he was about to do. He pressed end on the call. They were all fucked. He looked at Zoe and let out a heavy sigh.

"We know where Luscious is."

TO BE CONTINUED

# AN AMERICAN HUSTLER

Click the link to stay up to date: https://www.colehartsignature.com/an-american-hustler/

*Cole Hart*
SIGNATURE NOVELS

# THANK YOU

To our loyal Cole Hart Signature readers,

Cole Hart Signature is always growing and changing. Some of you have been following Cole Hart since the beginning of his career, while others have seen us go from Cole Hart Presents to Cole Hart Signature. Then there are our daily new supporters who've only known us for what we are as a company today. Despite our changes, how or when you became a fanatic, we want to kindly thank you for the support.

We appreciate all our Cole Hart Readers because without every single one of you, we wouldn't be the company we are today.

If this book is your first introduction to our company, welcome! And be sure to sign up for email list by click the link, http://bit.ly/2BtGCXH, and joining out text-mail list by texting Cole-HartSig to (855)231-5230. Cole Hart Signature also has a Facebook group where fans get to discuss the plot, characters, overall releases about their favorite book. If itching for new and interesting conversation, click the link, https://geni.us/ColeHartSignatureRead, to join today!

Lastly, Cole Hart Signature is always interested in partnering with aspiring authors, new or experienced, who thrive in the African Urban Fiction and Romance Fiction genre. If you're interested in joining our team, go to www. colehartsignature.com/submissions.

Once again, we truly appreciate all the support over the years.

Much Love,
   CHS

Made in the USA
Monee, IL
15 July 2021

73508952R00100